14

To ANNETTE,

So beautiful and wonderful in
every way
You're a girl who always lets the light
within you shine.
With strength and courage at every turn.
And so in those moments of life you
have shared. you brighten and
strengthen mine,

Taylor MacLean Saunders

CHRONICLES OF A STARCHASER

T. M. SAUNDERS

CHRONICLES OF A STARCHASER

iUniverse books may be ordered through booksellers or by contacting:

iUniverse LLC
1663 Liberty Drive
Bloomington, IN 47403
www.iuniverse.com
1-800-Authors (1-800-288-4677)

Because of the dynamic nature of the Internet, any web addresses or links contained in this book may have changed since publication and may no longer be valid. The views expressed in this work are solely those of the author and do not necessarily reflect the views of the publisher, and the publisher hereby disclaims any responsibility for them.

Any people depicted in stock imagery provided by Thinkstock are models, and such images are being used for illustrative purposes only. Certain stock imagery © Thinkstock.

ISBN: 978-1-4917-3725-5 (sc)
ISBN: 978-1-4917-3726-2 (hc)
ISBN: 978-1-4917-3727-9 (e)

Library of Congress Control Number: 2014910326

Printed in the United States of America.

iUniverse rev. date: 07/31/2014

Special thanks to Christine Lawrence *for her wonderful enthusiasm and perspective, and to* Jennifer Ng *for her always valuable assistance.*

In memory of Roy Ritchie (1937-2012) *and*
Linda Muirhead (1952-2012)

CONTENTS

ABBREVIATIONS, MEASURES, AND TERMS

AM (*anno mundi*): "in the year of the world"
astral-terrestrial, astral: alien
cubit: eighteen inches = 45.72 centimeters
cycle: one year
distributor: energy distribution pistol
elevat: elevator
furlong: .125 miles = .20 kilometers
Great Peace: a postapocalyptic period of a thousand years of peace
lumen-span: light-year
Old Earth: preapocalypse
time-keep: clock or wristwatch

PROLOGUE

1

Throughout ancient history, the Earth was corrupted.
Man was possessed by the ways of the Beast.
Civilizations that arose had fallen to dust
by way of their corruptions.
It came to be in the latter days that a Global Order arose and began
to reign with iniquity beyond any that had ever existed before it.
As it had been written, there were wars and rumors of wars;
Nation rose up against Nation; and when annihilation was
at hand, Divine intervention came from the heavens.
In the final hour, brimstone and fire scorched the Earth.
The Earth shook amid the millstones that were cast
down, and the Earth was then turned upon its axis.

2

The great Babylonia of empires had fallen.
The Great Book of Judgment was opened.
The chosen were given life for a thousand cycles,
and the Beast was chained for a thousand cycles,
having no further deceit upon the Nations.
Peace was instilled into the hearts and minds of men.
A new Eden on Earth had arisen and a
Divine Order had now come to pass.

3

*It was a time of Great Peace and prosperity, of good and plenty—
a time when the fruits of one's labors were rewarded tenfold.
It was a time when the lion lay down with the lamb,
when the serpent would not cause hurt, when all living
things shared a mutual trust in one another.
It was a time when man would no longer learn the
ways of war, nor be a slave unto another.
Death became a tale, for there was no death,
nor was there birth any longer.
It was a time of strength by flesh and bone,
not weakness by flesh and blood.*

4

*Come the time when the thousand cycles had ended,
the Great Beast was released from his chains.
Man was again left to his own accord, left with the
Divine laws that provided good unto him.
For a time all was good, and all was well,
but the Beast began to stir.
And though man possessed the wisdom of the ages and
held the laws of the Divine to pursue good and continue
existing in happiness, in his arrogance he believed he could
do better and began to impose his laws above all others.*

5

*Whilst man spread from the realm of his birth to the
reaching expanses of distant worlds, his ways became
increasingly corrupted to the ways of the Beast.
Temptations fed the will of men.
Ancient history was doomed to repeat.
As a warning to man's indiscretions, foreverance of life was
cut and quartered; it again became a time of flesh and blood.*

But these warnings remained unheeded.
New births occurred, and with those new generations,
the ways of Eden were soon forgotten.
Pruning hooks and ploughshares were beaten into swords.

<u>6</u>

Now, from the colonies of Earth, grows great discord.
The knowledge of the ages of the wise men has withered.
From close and from afar, wars and whispers of
wars begin to loom over man's existence.
But let it be known that the tribulations of man are of little
measure to what lies in the darkness of the expanse beyond.
For I had a vision and in it came Legions, and
the name of these Legions was Death.

The Warning
The late King Dafydd, the Orator
AM 7334 (AD 3330)

Starchaser, *noun*: a person who seeks cosmic adventure or dreams of outer-worldly exploration; one who pursues heavenly bodies.
Alpha & Omega Lexicon: Terms of Diction

ASPIRATIONS

I am Bishop Alexandrah Hays, and this is my story.

I am considered by most an Earthling in the true sense of the word. I was born and raised on Earth and grew up on my uncle Augustus's farm in King's Plain, Northern Antarctica, Loyal Commonwealth of Dafydd. Never having left the Earth and rarely leaving the small community where I grew up, I had seen myself as having no other choice in life than becoming a farmer. I didn't relish the thought. I had watched all my friends leave King's Plain to pursue their dreams, to pursue greater things in life, while I remained behind.

Being a farmer had its rewards—the planting, the nurturing of new life and the fruit of the harvests, and caring for the animals—but deep down it was not something that truly interested me. The things that interested me most were cosmic exploration and astral-terrestrial archaeology. For some inexplicable reason these were aspirations I had had since childhood. Whether playing in the nearby conifer forest of King's Plain Valley or in and around the family home, I always imagined being on some other world and discovering an amazing civilization.

I often explored it in my dreams or read about it in the Space Exploration Journals—the monthly publication of new discoveries from across the universe. Schooling for either, however, was expensive and was far beyond my uncle's financial capabilities.

The Loyal Space Corps was always an option. With the LSC there were no finances needed, but there were no guarantees either. I could take my training and sign up for extended voyages to neighboring galaxies, partake in planetary exploration, and visit ancient astral-terrestrial ruins, but once in, I could find myself serving in some other part of the Corps without choice, and patrolling a star system against galactic colony strife. It meant becoming a soldier. My uncle Augustus, though, did not wish to see his only surviving kin become a soldier.

"Bishop, it is not proper to entangle ourselves with the tribulations of outer worlds when we cannot even organize our own Earthly matters," he would state firmly.

His feelings toward cosmic travel were of comparable discontent.

"Space travel is unearthly, Bishop. If we were meant to fly out in the great beyond we would've been born with boosters up our backsides!" he would say. "All you'll find out there is the devil."

Like many, my uncle believed strongly that any life not of this Earth was a manifestation of the devil, some ungodly creation. I was never entirely convinced, but I rarely argued. Those times that I did, however, he would leave abruptly. On one heated occasion, I found his bedroom door ajar and saw him sitting on his bed doing his best to hold back his tears as he held a family picture.

I understood the real reason he didn't want me out there. Our family had been shrouded in tragedy. My aunt—my uncle's wife, Sinead—had been killed when a shuttle returning from Jupiter Station crashed. My cousin Arnold, my uncle's son, was killed when the LSC patrol ship on which he was serving was destroyed during a colonizing dispute. My own parents, my uncle's brother and sister-in-law, Kenneth and Hyacinthiah, were also subject to a similar demise. They had died when their hydroponics station was depressurized in an Andromeda separatist attack. I was barely two.

My uncle was firm in his belief that we had suffered through enough tragedies and that with our feet planted firmly on Earth, such tragedies would be well avoided. I always respected his wishes, but still, deep down, my calling was out there, among the stars. The LSC was not without its lingering temptation, but I wanted to pursue my ambitions in the freedom, safety, and guarantee of the civilian sector. A soldier I was not.

When I turned nineteen I left the farm to work at an information terminal in the Antarctica Shuttleport. The shuttleport was situated in Central Antarctica, in the middle of rolling cornfields. It was a magnificent structure consisting of a massive central operations tower, or "hub," as we called it. This hub was encircled by six sprawling ports, each with smaller observation and communications towers, located at the outermost point of the sprawling arms. These O and Cs were charged with the diligent task of guiding incoming and outgoing craft from the authority of the hub, and dispatching emergency services if required. It was a different routine from the farm, with strict rules and scheduling and the mandatory blue-and-white uniform, styled after the LSC. Men wore finely fitted tunics and breeches, and women wore fitted tunics with flared cuffs at the elbow and knee-length skirts—all rather striking and comfortable.

The shuttleport was twelve hundred furlongs from home, and considering the distance, I had a choice of staying in the cramped shuttleport staff lodgings or traveling to and from home by omnibus every morning and evening. As this daily travel was too costly and monotonous, I chose the former but would travel home once every two weeks to visit and spend a day or two partaking in the daily farming routine.

My excuse, to quell my uncle's concern of apparent abandonment of farming duties, was that half my wages from this new venture would help support the finances of the farm, which it did. But the truth of the matter was that I was determined to set aside the remaining half of my wages to take correspondence schooling in cosmic exploration and astral-terrestrial archaeology. This, however, was to be a long-term goal.

The shuttleport was as close as I got to space travel, and for five long, repetitious cycles, apart from the visits home, I did the same thing every day without change. Granted, the pay for an IT was good, and I met interesting people, many from the outer colonies, but for the most part, conversations were short, usually only consisting of the arrival and departure times of various shuttlecraft. So continued my monotonous life as an "it."

My half-hour lunch breaks provided some reprieve from the monotony of the day. The employee dining room was positioned on the north side of the shuttleport and had a view of shuttle pad E. From there I could watch a variety of incoming and outgoing craft. I always watched the ground crews running about and the guard personnel patrolling with vigilance, ready for an attack from some disgruntled Andromeda Galaxy separatist group. Everyone had something to do, and they ran about as if always behind in their duties. It all looked so exciting.

There were times, though, when I looked out the window and couldn't help but think that my goals were so far off—that this was as good as it was going to get for me. That this, for me, was all that life had to offer.

BIRTHDAY WISH

Earth
7 October AM 7454

It was my twenty-fourth birthday, and at lunch break, a few close shuttleport friends had arranged an unexpected party in the employee dining room for me.

My closest friend, Danikah, pulled her eyes away from the large, oval panel-viewer on the wall. It silently displayed LSC personnel marching captured Andromeda Galaxy separatists to a prison shuttle. Her eyes had been frequently glancing over at it since the start of the party.

"Well, go on, Bishop, make a wish!" she said in anticipation, her short black hair bouncing against her cheeks.

I chuckled and closed my eyes in an exaggerated act. A moment later I opened them and blew out the candles on a pink frosted cake. Everyone cheered.

"Well, what did you wish for?" Danikah cheerfully demanded.

"I think if she were to tell you, it wouldn't come true, now would it?" Edwin stated rhetorically in my defense. He was tall, his voice equally distinguishable above all others. His height made up for his lack of personality.

I kept my wish to myself. I didn't want anyone knowing that my wish was still my childhood aspiration of being a starchaser. The idea might seem laughable, I thought. I was silently thankful for Edwin's defense.

A loud beep sounded. The panel-viewer images were suddenly interrupted. The words *Incoming Communication* scrolled across the panel, followed by *Loyal Space Corps, Saturn Station*. Numbers counted down from five. It looked to be an official alert message. Then the face of a young, dark-haired, square-jawed man wearing a white LSC tunic appeared on the viewer. I held my hand to my face in disbelief.

"Charley!" I exclaimed.

"Hey, happy birthday, Blondie-Blue!" he said to me. It was Charles Avery, my ex-boyfriend of three cycles who left me and the ASP communication services to attend the Loyal Space Corps Cadet College. "Blondie-Blue" was his nickname for me. On first seeing me—noting my hair and eyes and not knowing my name—that's what he called me, and it fondly stuck.

"Thanks, Charley." I chuckled, pulling my hair back and over my shoulder.

"Sorry I don't have a gift for you!"

There were several seconds of delay between our messages, making conversation awkward.

"This is perfect," I replied, still surprised at seeing him.

"How are things at the ASP?" he asked.

"Good," I replied. "There's been a lot of new guard personnel added since the recent Andromeda attacks, but everything's good."

"We're safe and secure!" shouted Danikah happily.

"Hi, guys!" he said to everyone. "I see you've started the party without me!"

"You're late!" joked Danikah. "We had to!"

"I know, sorry about that! I'd have messaged sooner, but they've got me pretty busy here!"

"Have they made you an officer yet?" asked Danikah.

"No," Charley said, smiling, as he looked at me and tugged at his sleeve that displayed two yellow circles. "Just a grunt communications corporal a few months ago. Moons, as we call them! Do you have a private audiocomm there?" he then asked, before the delay enabled Danikah to take over the conversation.

Danikah handed one to me with a smirk, as if she knew it would be requested. I pressed the privacy button, held it to my ear, and walked toward the viewer.

"How's your uncle Augustus?" Charley asked.

"He's fine. Stubborn as always," I replied.

"That's him." He laughed. "You look perfect, Bishop," he added with hesitation.

"You too."

"I know we're not—oh, thanks. It's just the uniform, that's all." He laughed again.

"Go ahead, Charley," I said. The message delay was difficult to adjust to.

"Um, I know we're not together anymore, and I know we agreed to continue our lives apart and chase our own directions, but I had to see you."

"I'm glad you did, Charley." I turned back to see how closely my friends were listening in. All wore stupid grins on their faces, intently wondering what Charley's private words to me were.

"I'm sure there are others out there," I said quietly.

8

"Not like you, Bishop."

His words were sincere, as if he was regretting his decision to leave me for the LSC.

Danikah suddenly put her chin on my shoulder and peered up at Charley, attempting to listen in on his words. She gave an exaggerated and ridiculous smile and fluttered her eyelashes.

I chuckled; so did Charley. "How's Saturn Station?" I asked, attempting to sway the intimate conversation of regrets from Danikah's invasive ears.

"Busy. We're heading out to—" The panel-viewer blacked out and the communication went static. Everyone around me gasped. We stared, believing that was the end of the communication. I was about to take the audiocomm away when the panel-viewer reestablished its link. "Sorry," continued Charley. "That was the censor. All I can tell you is I'm heading out, so I don't know when I'll be able to send you a message again. They've been keeping contact limited. Whenever I see you again, I'll probably be a guard sergeant—"

"Ten seconds, corporal Avery," a firm voice informed him.

Charley looked disappointed—not just from the time left but also from the probability of becoming a guard sergeant. Becoming a guardsman—a frontline soldier—was something he'd never wanted.

"There's more I want to say, more I'd like to tell you, but I have to go."

"Be safe, Charley."

"I will, Blondie-Blue. Happy twenty-fourth! Love you always!" he said quickly and touched the viewer as if to touch my face. It then went black. *End Communication* appeared.

"Love you too," I whispered. The panel-viewer returned to the horrors of the separatist reports. I turned my back and continued with the festivities that had been put on hold for me.

The get-together was short; spanning only the half-hour lunch break. I was sitting down when the return bell called, my thoughts now mostly of Charley. My friends wished me a happy birthday and then quickly dropped their food and drinks on the table and scurried from the room, as if being late meant forfeiting their limited and stagnant careers.

I wasn't too concerned about returning to my terminal; after all, it was my birthday; such as it was. I remained in my chair and looked out the window at an incoming shuttle. The high-frequency pitch from its engines violently rattled the windows. It was the S-33, fondly known as the "green onion," and it was as it sounded: green and shaped like an onion—short and fat. Landing fins hugged the underside and reached its midsection; from the midsection fixed to the fins were long hyperlaunch antennae that measured to the point of the hull. From the point of the hull were the long communication and deflector array antennae. The S-33 was clumsy in appearance and was different from the typically tall, sleek, pointed, cylindrical shuttles that towered nearby. Slowly it came and settled down. The ground crews were running about as usual.

"Ah, the green onion," said an amused flight captain, dressed in his tidy blue uniform. "They don't build 'em like that anymore."

"No," I agreed rather distantly.

"She's a rare one that; most of 'em have been taken out of civilian service and refitted as light battleships by the Space Corps. Worth their weight in victory in the Andromeda wars. They're really maneuverable despite how they look landing in an atmosphere."

"Have you piloted one before?" I asked.

He smiled proudly. "I am the pilot—one of them. This'll be my shift. I head out as soon as she's ready for departure."

An announcement came over the intercom. "Captain Waverley, report to departure pad E seventeen."

"That's me," he said.

"Have fun," I said, not knowing what else to say.

"Always do!" he replied happily and dashed out of the room. All around me was just another reminder of where I wanted to be. I glanced down at a magazine on the table. It was the *Space Exploration Journal*. The headlines and moving images on its cover transformed into various topics.

> *Deep Space Discoveries*
> Astral-Terrestrial Ruins Found on Darkawhah, Zechariah Galaxy: *Who Were These Beings?*
> Star-Charging Theory Deemed Impossible
> Oxygen-Producing Crystals Discovered on Mobius
> Sun Suddenly Dies before Astronomers' Eyes: *What Will This Mean for the System's Life-Sustaining Planets?*
> Professor Charlemagne Creeggan Speaks about the Tecton Field
> Claire Carter Celebrated: *The Missing Astral-Planetary Geologist Remembered, Past Articles Reviewed*

The topics brought absolute delight, but the cheeriness quickly disappeared from me as I looked over at a custodial drone that whizzed past. I suddenly thought better of my starchasing and sat up.

"I won't get anywhere in life just sitting around dreaming," I uttered to myself. Right then I was fixed on joining the LSC and the risk of becoming a soldier. The enlistment station was located at terminal C and wasn't far. "Space Corps, here I come." Maybe I would get to see Charley.

As I exited the dining room, exuding determination, I was struck down by a man running past. We both crashed violently to the floor.

"I'm terribly sorry, miss," he said quickly, picking himself up.

I got to my feet and rubbed the back of my neck from the whiplash. The man put his hands on my shoulders and peered into my eyes. He was handsome. He reminded me a little of Charley, but older and with short, dark-blond hair. I remained speechless as I stared into his unique blue-green eyes.

"Are you all right?" he asked.

"Yeah, I think so," I answered, uncertain. "Who are you?"

"The Commander," he answered, still with his hands on my shoulders, looking at me to see if I was okay.

I glanced at his clothes. They were bright white and almost resembled an LSC uniform, but without insignia or any form of rank. "This area's for shuttleport personnel. What are you doing here?" I demanded while trying to regain my composure.

"I'm looking for my ship—"

A thundering voice interrupted his answer. "Don't move!" it shouted.

We both looked over. An ASP guardsman was running toward us from the far end of the hall and pointing a distributor at us. I didn't recognize him. He obviously didn't recognize me. He must have been one of the new reinforcements.

"Both of you, on the floor!" he ordered nervously. "Now!"

Three hovering security drones surrounded us.

"Hold on!" said the Commander firmly as he raised his hands.

Uneasy with the Commander's movement, the guardsman suddenly pulled the trigger. A blue beam flashed. I fell back, and the Commander caught me. I was completely immobilized and numb. All I could do was watch and listen.

"What have you done?" he cried as he knelt and gently guided me to the floor, staring angrily at the guardsman.

"You're wanted for invasion of premises and will be held under the Separatist Conspirators Act until this all gets sorted!"

The Commander touched a small gray device on his belt, which gave a brief, high-frequency pitch. The three hovering security drones wobbled and then fell to the floor.

The guardsman watched in awe, looking at the drone to his right and then the other to his left. He looked back at the Commander and swallowed nervously. I could feel anger radiating from the Commander as he stood up and walked toward the guardsman.

The guard's hands shook violently as he tried to sight a clear shot. "*Sir,* stop where you are," he ordered.

The Commander continued toward him.

"Sir, *please,*" the guardsman pleaded.

His words seemed to fall upon deaf ears. The Commander continued forward without any regard to his own being.

Tightening his grip on the distributor, the guardsman squeezed the trigger. The trigger clicked. Nothing happened.

With ease, the Commander grabbed the distributor from the guardsman's hand. "You need to rearm it," he growled while cocking it. It gave a recharging whine as he looked at its intensity setting.

The guardsman simply watched while shaking and whimpering. The Commander grabbed the guardsman's collar while glaring into his eyes. The guardsman fainted. The Commander let go and left him to drop haphazardly to the floor as he tossed the distributor aside and hurried toward me. I began to convulse.

"Come on," he said as he picked me up and carried me off.

I then lost consciousness.

THE COMMANDER

I awoke to see a blurry image of someone's face. The face appeared to be upside down and was moving from side to side. It took a moment for my vision to clear and put things in perspective. I was lying on my back; the face was staring over me. It was that of the strange man who had run into me on my way out of the dining room. It was the Commander.

"Hello!" he said cheerfully. He bent farther forward and looked closely into my eyes and then backed away.

It took an additional moment to gather my thoughts and realize my surroundings were unfamiliar—a finely polished and luminous white room filled with strange apparatuses.

"Where am I?" I asked groggily. I felt horribly sick. The Commander seemed to sense this.

"Take it easy. You're aboard the Dee-Dee. You were in the revitalization chamber. You're lucky. That distributor setting was far too high for someone of your size. It could have killed you."

I sat up slowly. The Commander assisted me.

"The Dee-Dee? What's that?" I asked.

"My ship," he answered, as if I should know. "I found it!" He turned in half a circle and held out his arms.

I then threw up.

"My floor!" he suddenly yelped.

"Sorry" was all I could muster.

"Feel better?"

"Yeah."

"Good," he said quickly. He continued as if it didn't matter, as if nothing had happened. "Terminal E 2, not C 2. How was I to know terminal C was a secured area?"

"Terminal C is restricted for Space Corps ships," I informed him.

"Well, see, there you go, then. I mean, have a sign or something. It'll save every Harry, Dick, and Tom from . . . or is it Tom, Dick, and Harry?" he mused. "I can never remember." He shook his head. "Doesn't matter. These new-style Earth letters get confusing. If you don't remember that extra *thingy* on the E, then you're in a real slek."

"A what?"

"A slek! It's like a . . ." He paused a moment, pondering. "Only . . . not."

I then threw up again.

The Commander paused and then blurted suddenly, "You done tossing your pink lunch on my clean floor?"

"I hope so," I said, feeling instantly better, for the moment.

"Not to worry, 'cause there's lots of room left . . . Anyway, once I'm done here, I'll take you back."

"Take me back? Where exactly are we?" I asked as I stood up.

"Come on."

"What about my . . . lunch?"

"It'll be absorbed," he said, without any further care.

I followed him toward a door that had a downward-pointing triangular window. It offered a view into what looked to be an emerald green forest. The door silently slid open and we entered a massive garden of exotic-looking trees and plants, some with flamboyant flowers. Directly ahead was a wide hallway and another doorway situated at the end similar to the one we were exiting.

Above was a vaulted and bright white ceiling. Light appeared to emanate from it with no signs of luminescent fixtures. It was as an even glow of sunlight on a clear day—it was unlike anything I had ever seen.

We stepped behind a railing and gently ascended on an elevat. Another was positioned nearby. To have two in close proximity would seem to indicate the crew was abundant, but there appeared to be no one else about. Apart from the Commander and me, it was completely silent.

We quickly reached a balcony overlooking the garden. Before I had a chance to view it completely, the Commander led the way into what looked to be the command deck. It was, as the rest, a brilliantly polished and luminous white. I wandered around and looked at a round, table-like console located in the center of the room. It was void of buttons, knobs, switches, and blinking lights that adorned any console on an Earth or colony ship; this was sleek.

"Welcome to the bridge," he said proudly. "You might know it better as a command deck, but I call it the bridge." He pressed a shaded circle on the console. A transparent image with several waving lines appeared over its center.

"Where's your crew?" I asked, still in a weakened state.

"No crew," he replied while staring at the floating image.

A commander of a ship with no crew to command? Strange, I thought.

"Why are there no windows in your ship?" *If this is a ship there should be windows,* I thought.

"There are windows; I just have them covered."

"Why?"

"It's safer that way."

"Safer? Why's it safer?" I voiced with concern.

"Because the Dee-Dee's orbiting Phoebus, your sun," he replied flatly. "That's how I regenerate the power supply."

"You're *star-charging* your ship?"

"In a manner."

"But star-charging is only a theory, a theoretical invention not in actual practice," I stated firmly. "It doesn't exist."

"Does here," he assured.

"Oh," I responded, and thought a moment. "Phoebus? That's an ancient name for the sun, one that's barely known and never used."

"Not since long before the Great Peace," he said.

Who is he? I wondered.

"You're not exactly from here, are you?"

"Nope," he answered.

Was he a separatist?

"Are you . . . from one of the outer galactic colonies?" I asked reluctantly.

"Nope," he answered again.

"Then where are you from, exactly?"

"Oh! Come on, Dee-Dee!" he suddenly bellowed at the floating image.

"Why's your ship called Dee-Dee?"

"Because it's named after the Displacement Drive—DD."

"Displacement Drive? What's that?"

He touched a shaded square on the console. "That, right there." He pointed out.

I looked in the intended direction to discover there were two narrow cylinders within an alcove, one lowering into the floor, and the other rising into the ceiling. A small illuminated golden sphere appeared to hover between them. An occasional flicker of white light emanated from its core. I was inexplicably drawn toward it.

"I've never heard of it," I said softly as I walked around it and stared in fascination. I became relaxed beyond description.

"You wouldn't. It's its own design. One of a kind!" he declared proudly.

"What does it do?" I asked in an almost hypnotic trance.

"Makes you go really fast."

"How fast?"

He snapped his fingers. "Blink of an eye."

I was startled by his snap and turned. He was pointing his finger at me.

"How long does it take you to travel across your solar system?" he asked.

"The Terra Mater system? It depends on the ship—the fastest? Through a hyperlaunch ring? Half a day."

"Half a blink of an eye for the Dee-Dee," he declared quickly.

"That's impossible," I expressed in disbelief. "It's thousands upon thousands of lumen-spans."

"That's right," the Commander agreed. "The Dee-Dee can travel millions of lumen-spans in a matter of moments."

"You're . . ." I paused and stared at him in wonderment. There was only one other possibility. Admittedly, I was jumping to a grandiose conclusion, but I thought if he was not of an Earthly or colony realm, then he must be from an astral-terrestrial one. He had to be. It would explain the ship! "You're not exactly human . . . are you?" I asked with extreme hesitation.

"Well, yes—er, no—er, well, I'm *humanesque*," he replied.

18

"You're an astral-terrestrial!" I stated excitedly.

"Nnnot necessarily an astral-terrestrial in the sense that I'm, well, an *astral-terrestrial*. Suffice it to say I'm . . . *humanoid.*" He frowned at the floating image. "Actually, I'm *very* annoyed," he added, passing his hand back and forth through the waving lines. He then looked at me. "I suppose this surprises you—seeing how your Loyal Space Corps has been exploring its own and neighboring galaxies for centuries and still hasn't encountered any astral life of any way, shape, form, or description? Apart from a few moldy ruins."

"Uh, yeah," I replied.

"What gave it away, anyway?" He turned to a reflective but distorting convex metallic panel on the console and began contorting his expression. "It's the ears, isn't it? They're too big."

I looked at him strangely for a moment and began to smile as he pulled on his ears.

"Or perhaps it's that they're too small."

"You look really normal, actually," I said.

He turned and looked at me and puffed out his cheeks. He clearly had a jovial persona.

I chuckled and turned to the sphere, staring in wonderment. This Displacement Drive was indeed astral-terrestrial. However it worked, the science of it all was obviously far beyond my understanding and no doubt beyond the understanding of many scientists who would be eager to study it.

"Don't keep staring into it," the Commander ordered. "It'll rot your brain."

I pulled my head back and turned. He had a grin and was looking at me from the corner of his eye. From that I immediately determined that he was joking. "Where *are* you from, exactly?"

"You sure ask a lot of questions, don't you?"

"Wouldn't you?" I jousted.

The Commander tilted his head and raised an eyebrow in partial agreement. "I have a question for *you, Bishop Alexandrah Hays.*"

"How'd you know my name?"

"I scanned your shuttleport data files before you threw up on my floor."

"Oh."

"Happy birthday, by the way."

"Thanks. What's your question then?"

"Well," he said, frowning. "Bishop, Bishop, Bishop," he uttered under his breath while holding his chin. "Why *Bishop?*" he blurted indiscriminately. "That's an Old Earth clergyman's title."

"Well . . . my parents gave it to me," I said.

"Oh. *Right.* Good answer!" he replied; then, deeply thinking as he stared at the image floating over the console, he added, "How unusual."

"Perhaps," I agreed reluctantly. "My uncle was never sure why they chose it. It—"

"I meant Phoebus, your Sun. It's unusual."

"Oh." I frowned. "So what's *your* name?"

"I told you—the Commander."

"That's a title, a rank. You must have a name?"

"Nope, just the Commander."

"A commander of what?"

"Of what was and is no more." He swiftly walked over to a large shaded square located on the wall and slammed his palm against it.

Two curved panels began to slide away from each other above a forward console and provided a panoramic view into the black star-specked expanse of space.

GLIMPSES

I walked forward and stood in awe of the sight before me. If the Commander's intention was to change the subject and distract me from my incessant request that he tell me his name, it worked.

The stars began to move sideways; the view began to shift toward Phoebus, the flaming sun of the Terra Mater system. Soon, the motion stopped. Nothing but the sun could be seen. A yellow flare unexpectedly erupted from the surface and dissipated as it approached the ship. The sight should have been frightful, but I remained complacent. *Some powerful star-shield must be protecting us,* I thought. *Otherwise at this distance we'd be vaporized in seconds—or at the very least blinded.*

The Commander stood beside me and gently pressed a shaded circle on the console. A swift swishing sound followed. Moments later an elongated silver capsule drifted into view and turned end over end toward the flaming sun. We watched silently as the capsule slowly traveled farther and farther away.

I looked at the Commander. "What is that?"

"An old friend," he answered solemnly.

I looked at the Sun once more. The capsule became noticeably smaller.

"She wanted to visit Earth once more before she died," the Commander continued. "Her last wish was to be cremated by Phoebus."

"Was she from Earth?"

"Yes."

A somber silence fell upon us as a swirling flare swept across and swallowed the capsule.

"We traversed the stars for a very long time."

"How long?" I asked politely.

"Oh, let's see now," the Commander said, thinking. "It would be-e-e . . . 180 cycles—181 to be exact."

"A hundred and eighty cycles?" I said in disbelief. "You don't look that old."

"Thank you." He smiled.

"How old are you?"

"In Earth cycles?" he queried. "About 4,800 or so, I guess. Give or take." He nodded in agreement with his own answer. "I've lost count."

"Four *thousand?*" I said. "No way. You look like you're only . . . forty."

"Thirty-nine, actually," he confided in jest. "I've not been ready to commit to forty yet."

I smiled at the Commander's wit. I looked away and paused. "That's . . . *ancient,*" I stressed. "You must've seen it all. On Earth, I mean—before the Great Peace."

"Not all. But I've seen a few interesting things when I've visited."

"Like what?" I asked enthusiastically.

The Commander mused over his past journeys as if in his many cycles there was much to choose from. "Well, I expect much of Old Earth has been lost to you over the Great Peace, but I saw the siege of Troy," he declared.

"Really? I know that one. Was it true there was a big wooden horse?" I asked even more enthusiastically.

The Commander looked around as if there might be someone listening. He leaned toward me. "I promised I would never say," he said quietly, which seemed in some strange cryptic way to mean yes.

"What else?" I wanted to know.

He thought carefully. "The construction of the Great Wall?"

I shook my head unknowingly.

"No? Hmm . . . saw the eruption of Mount Vesuvius and the destruction of Pompeii."

I shook my head again.

"Met Napoleon during his defeat at Waterloo," he said with a strange, unfamiliar accent and his hand held to his chest in what seemed to be an associated pose.

I chuckled at his apparent impersonation. All were indeed fragments of Old Earth history lost to the Great Peace.

"Don't know those," I replied.

"Saw the rise and fall of what was the New World Order and witnessed the onslaught of the Apocalypse . . . watched the first Earth ship break the lumen-span barrier . . ."

I was flabbergasted; I stood in amazement. "What else? What's . . . out there?" I asked with great infatuation.

"You mean *out there?* In the universe?"

"Yeah."

"Oh, well, there's civilizations lost, others triumphant, colors not seen, sounds unheard . . . places so obscure that it would turn science upside down and inside out—places beyond all description, really. The wonders never cease, that's for sure."

I looked toward the sun. I was aghast by the Commander's information. Sadness came over me as I saw another flare explode. It reminded me of the capsule. "Who was she?"

The Commander smiled. "Claire . . . a very brave little girl when I found her. Nine cycles of age. She was the only survivor of an Andromeda-bound Civil Earth Fleet. She survived on a half-destroyed supply freighter for over two cycles. I returned her home to her relatives on Earth. I then met her again forty cycles later. She was living in a small village on Tarcees."

"That's in the Andromeda Galaxy."

"Yes. Tarcees was where she and her family were going when she was a girl. She followed in her family's footsteps and became an astral-planetary geologist."

"Claire . . ." That name sounded familiar. "You don't mean Claire Carter, do you? *That* astral-planetary geologist?"

"Yes," replied the Commander.

"She wrote the most amazing articles in the antiquated volumes of the *Space Exploration Journals*," I voiced with intrigue.

"I know."

"But she went missing," I returned with bewilderment.

"No."

"Yes, she did."

"No, she went with me."

"Wow," I uttered in fascination.

"Mm," returned the Commander calmly.

"What was her reason?"

"Well, my sparkling personality, of course."

I laughed. "No, really, she must have had a reason to walk away from her fame."

"She was angry with the Astral-Geosciences Administration for ignoring her warnings of an impending quake on Tarcees.

When it occurred, over two hundred thousand colonists died. So instead of remaining and rubbing it in their faces, she left."

"Wow." I paused. "You're . . . alone then."

"Now I am," he said softly. "But you're never alone when you traverse the stars," he added optimistically and smiled.

I smiled in return. His answer was sincere, but I detected an inkling of loneliness despite his cheerful tone.

The Commander turned and walked away. "I'll take you back now. I hope you don't mind walking. I think it's best I land a ways from your shuttleport. They'll still be looking for me . . . and for you."

"What do I tell them?" I asked in bewilderment.

"I don't care what you tell them. Tell them a big green astral-terrestrial with five green eyes took you away," he spoke facetiously. "Get them all stirred up. They need that—gives them something else to do. Give them a common enemy." He began to mumble. "Instead of killing each other pointlessly, they can unite in harmony with a common purpose."

I remained silent and reflected upon my situation. I was in a spaceship; I was in space; I was before an astral-terrestrial who had witnessed historic happenings on Earth and could travel impossible distances—to other places, to other worlds . . . *He* was an adventurer. *I* was an adventurer at heart . . . My birthday wish had come true. My childhood aspirations were suddenly before me. True, I had only known this commander—*the* Commander—for a few short minutes, but I felt, in some strange way, as though I had known him all my life. He was comfortable to be around. Trusting. Fun. He lacked the stressed qualities of everyone I knew on Earth—including my uncle. I was presented with a possible opportunity.

"I don't want to go back," I said suddenly.

"What do you mean?"

"I don't want to go back!" I repeated firmly.

"What about your friends, your family, your life? Your life's on that little blue marble."

Those words hit a chord. It was truth that hurt. "My life's going nowhere!" I snapped and turned away.

"Oh, here we go," the Commander uttered under his breath. "Don't say that," he said sympathetically and walked toward me.

"It's true!" I cried and then turned and looked directly up at him. "Do you know what I've wanted ever since I was little?"

"No, but I feel as though I'm about to," he jeered.

"I've wanted so much to travel the stars, to see what's out there! I've wanted to explore astral ruins, other planets, other solar systems, other—"

"It's dangerous," the Commander interrupted.

"Of course it's dangerous!" I exclaimed. "And I don't care! Won't you get bored traveling the stars alone with no one to talk to?"

"Maybe, but . . . but . . ." he floundered for an excuse. "You're a guy; I'm a girl!" he said hastily. "People will talk!"

"*You're* a guy, *I'm* a girl," I corrected him.

"That's what I said, wasn't it?" he retorted with certainty.

"You're over *four thousand cycles old*. I'm *twenty-four*! What's to talk about? Do the math!" I exclaimed. "You're too old to be my boyfriend!"

"Well, yeah." He nodded. "You raise a valid point there, and—"

"Well?"

"You don't realize the full extent of what's out there," the Commander stressed. "Sure there's the amazing, the fascinating, and the unexplored. But there's also a whole other realm too. There's the horrific, the evil, the demonic—and that's only the dawning!" He snapped his fingers and pointed at me. "Have you ever been amidst a Karshashkalip?"

"No." I frowned. "I don't even know what a . . . Karshashka-whatever is."

"No! And believe me, sister—you don't want to," he informed me bluntly.

"If you're trying to scare me, it's not working," I declared.

He sighed and wandered away. He stared out the panoramic window. "No. Obviously not."

"What about Claire?" I queried sharply.

"What about Claire?" returned the Commander, briefly glancing back at me.

"*She* traveled with you."

"That was different. Claire was . . ." Sadness loomed over him. "Claire was different," he finished.

Claire had been close to him.

"How?"

The Commander was about to answer. But there was nothing to say. He closed his mouth and stared thoughtfully back through the window. He pondered carefully. "It . . . *could* work," he muttered and nodded. "A trial run . . . a taste . . . I mean, it certainly wouldn't be the first time, and I mean . . ."

As I overheard his optimistic mutterings, I grinned.

"You . . . I . . . except—we'd have to make a few ground rules," the Commander said as he stared at me. "But sure. Why not?" he announced. "Welcome aboard!"

I jumped in excitement and gave him an unexpected hug. It was going to be an adjustment, not only for him, but for me too. My five cycles working at the Antarctica Shuttleport had been certainly monotonous, but it was routine, a familiar routine, and now who knew what the future held in store.

And I would have to tell my uncle . . .

HOME

The Dee-Dee silently and gently hovered over a rocky plateau. A ramp began to open. Daylight and a gust of warm Antarctic air invited itself inward.

The Dee-Dee was peculiar compared to vessels from Earth and its many interstellar colonies. It was a massive triangular configuration and reflected the surroundings like liquid mercury.

As we stepped away, the ramp raised, and before my very eyes the Dee-Dee began to warble and transform into an additional rocky shelf on the plateau.

"Out of sight, out of mind," said the Commander. "Lead the way, Bishop Hays."

And so I did, down the plateau and through a vast golden wheat field that stretched out across the horizon. This was the Hays family farm, extending as far as the eye could see. A mild gust of wind caused the sheaves to glisten in the bright sunlight and elegantly dance around us.

A short distance away, an aged, saucer-like crop protector drone hovering over the sheaves was busy with its multiple long arms, electro-zapping various insects in midflight. Others doing the same were dotted about in the distance. It was an occurrence familiar to most farms on the Antarctic plains, and I always found them unsettling contraptions, even though I had spent hours repairing them. The Commander seemed unaffected by their presence.

"I remember when all this was covered in ice and snow," the Commander reminisced. "How things change over time."

We proceeded down a hill and toward an opening in a wall of piled stones that bordered the family apple orchard. The trees were immense, the trunks gnarled from age. As we walked under the canopy of trees and through lush emerald green grass, a mechanized buzz emanated from above. Suddenly a small, cylindrical harvester drone descended from between the branches with a basketful of large red apples. They were friendlier in appearance than the crop protectors.

The Commander stopped and stared at the drone. "Oh! Thank you," he said as he nonchalantly plucked one of the apples from its basket.

The drone gave a series of beeps as if irritated and buzzed around us.

"We shouldn't be here while the harvesters are working," I informed him.

As we hurried, the Commander dusted off the apple on his sleeve and bit into it. It had obviously been a long while since he had bitten into an Earth-grown apple. The apples were just as juicy and delicious as they always were. We watched cautiously as other harvester drones descended without warning and flew past us with their baskets full; the odd one giving a blare of disgruntled beeps and buzzes.

We soon exited the orchard and followed a well-worn path, shaded by trees that led to a plank bridge over a stream. The path continued along the stream and beside the familiar old windmill and millpond. Six white swans that always congregated there floated peacefully on the dark water, unaffected by our presence. We soon come upon the Hays family house a short distance away. Only the top portion of the peak could be seen amongst the tall oak trees that surrounded it.

On our approach, an old friend bounded toward us and cheerfully barked. It was Sebastian, a rather large mongrel. I had grown up with Sebastian, and he was always loyal and protective of me.

"Oh, this is no good," the Commander declared grimly while chewing and staring at Sebastian. "That's one more ground rule I forgot to mention."

"What?"

He swallowed. "No pets. Period! If you've come for *that*, then you're not coming at all."

"Don't you like dogs?"

"Oh, I like dogs fine, but they have this nasty habit of placing their noses in various places."

"Well, don't worry; I'm not here for him."

Sebastian came up to me with his tail wagging vigorously.

"Hello, Sebastian," I said, hugging him affectionately. "Uncle would be lost without you, wouldn't he? Hmm?"

Sebastian looked up at the Commander and gave a gruff, welcoming bark.

"Hello . . . *dog*," he reluctantly acknowledged.

Sebastian circled around and nudged his nose into the Commander's leg.

"See what I mean?" he said.

"He likes you," I commented. "He doesn't like everyone. He usually growls."

"Lucky me," he returned dryly.

He looked down at the panting dog that appeared to be smiling up at him. He then looked at the half-eaten apple in his hand and tossed it into the grass. Sebastian ran over and instantly began devouring it.

"Must have worms," the Commander muttered.

"Nooo, don't say that," I chuckled. "He's actually healthy for his longevity."

"Oh?" the Commander questioned. "How old is he?"

"Almost eighty cycles. He was my uncle's when he was a child."

Farther along was the barn. The Commander's attention became suddenly fixated. He broke away from the path and toward the wooden rail fence that surrounded the barn. It was obvious what was drawing his attention.

"That's Morganah," I said.

Morganah was a peacefully mannered mare, ever pleasant to be around and work with. She was the last of the Hays family work animals, having been replaced by drones and machines. She casually watched while chewing a mouthful of grass.

"Hello, girl," said the Commander while petting her nose gently.

Morganah blinked calmly. The Commander seemed to connect with her and lose himself. He quietly whispered to her. A crowing rooster soon broke his connection.

"Well, let's go," he said.

"Hail greetings, Miss Bishop," a monotone voice hollered.

A mechanical—a synthetic human—exited from the barn with a bucket of oats in hand and made a hurried approach.

"Hello Servitude!" I said. Servitude was the family slave. He had been around for as long as I could remember, and, with some affection, I always referred to him as a "he," though like all mechanicals, he was genderless. He was decommissioned

LSC property with a slight personality adjustment, his gray exoskeleton now heavily weatherworn and abused.

"Servitude heard your voice and came to investigate. I did not expect your return yet, Miss Bishop." He picked a small, mauve daisy from the grass.

"Neither did I," I said, noticing another acquired scuff across his dirty gray chest plate. "How are you?"

"Servitude is fully functional and upright." He gave a limited smile and offered the daisy. *"Birthday salutations, Miss Bishop."*

"Thank you, Servitude." I chuckled and took the meek offering. "Where's Uncle?"

"Master Augustus is harvesting in the south field."

I was somewhat relieved. I was reluctant to tell him in person of my decision.

"Shall Servitude send for him?"

"No," I said forcefully, "I'll leave a messager." I didn't want to be witness to my uncle's disappointment. A messager was my way out.

"As you wish, Miss Bishop," he replied, adding in a low, mysterious whisper, *"And who is your companion? Another fine boyfriend, I expect?"*

The Commander looked at me with a strange expression.

"N-no," I stuttered. "This is the Commander. Just a friend."

"Commander?" he said, almost surprised as if recollecting past service protocols. *"I am Servitude. How do you do, sir?"* He offered to shake the Commander's hand through the fence, which the Commander did with some reluctance.

"Just peachy," replied the Commander flatly.

"Most excellent, sir. A parcel arrived for you this morning, Miss Bishop. I placed it at the back door for your uncle."

"Who's it from?" I asked.

"It does not say."

"Thank you, Servitude."

"You are welcome." Servitude led Morganah away with the bucket. *"Come, Morganah. It is time for shoeing."*

"Any more drones, pets, or slaves going to sprout from the woodwork on the Hays' family dwelling?" asked the Commander in a mildly obnoxious way as we left.

"We can visit the *sheeps* if you like," I answered smartly.

"Sheeps? No, I'll pass on the sheeps, thanks."

We entered through a wrought iron gate surrounded by tall majestic ferns and onto a paved stone walkway leading to the house. Ivy hugged the stone walls, and yellow roses framed the wooden-crisscross-paned windows and reached the weathered thatch roof. I loved that old house and the childhood adventures I'd had within it.

As Servitude had said, a parcel sat on the doorstep, a tiny box wrapped in pink paper with my name printed on it. I picked it up. "Wonder who it's from," I whispered as I tried to open the door only to find it locked. I sighed. "I don't have my code-key."

"Let me," the Commander volunteered. He removed the small gray device from his belt that he had used at the ASP and held it to the access panel.

"What is that, anyway?"

"It's a disruptor," he replied as it gave a brief high-frequency pitch. The door popped ajar.

"One of my handy little gadgets." He smiled.

I entered as the Commander stood at the doorway and stared outward into the garden.

"You can come in," I quickly welcomed him.

As he stepped ambiguously into the large, dim kitchen, Sebastian sat patiently outside. The Commander walked past the large kitchen table and began looking at various old kitchen implements dotted around. There was the iron grain mill, the stave barrel butter churn that sat in the corner, and large clay pots for pickling. Many of these items were still used.

"Gosh, I haven't seen one of these for ages," he uttered, picking up a corkscrew. He looked at it intently and smiled while rotating the handle with his finger. "Get what you need and hurry up," he prodded.

I hurried down a hallway and ran up the wide set of stairs, almost tripping twice, and down a long dark hall toward my room. It was the seventh door on the left. It was dark, the windows covered by the large trees outside.

I immediately grabbed an old pink duffel bag from my wardrobe, first tossing in my mysterious gift, and then moving on to clothes I thought I might need. *Who knows? I might have go somewhere dirty; I might have to dress up!* My favorites were in my shuttleport lodging, and there was no chance of returning for them. *I'll make do,* I thought. I haphazardly crammed in whatever else I thought I could use. It was a hopeless jumble to be sorted later.

In my frantic grabbing, I knocked some books off a shelf. They fell to the floor with a loud series of thumps.

"You all right?" the Commander's shouted, his voice muffled.

"Yeah," I replied.

"Well, hurry up before Antarctica freezes over again!"

"Almost!" I replied quickly.

Lastly, I took a messager that was conveniently sitting on the bookshelf in front of me—a small thin disk. I snagged a momentary glance at a framed collage of pictures of my parents, Charley, and my uncle and me with Sebastian that was on the same shelf.

I looked at my uncle. His gray hair, brought on by financial stresses of the farm, contrasted his otherwise still youthful appearance. Deep down it felt wrong to leave as I was, but it was just easier not to tell him in person. If I did, I would see his unhappiness about my decision and I might change my mind. I couldn't risk it when I was so close to my dream. I did my best to ignore these conflicting surges of feelings and snatched the collage from the shelf, quickly shoved it into my duffel bag and continued downstairs.

I found the Commander still in the kitchen, studying a cluster of grapes in a bowl. Before I had a chance to instruct otherwise, he picked one and put it in his mouth. The anticipation of its taste quickly changed as he began to chew. He uttered a groan of disgust and pulled the grape from his mouth. He then noticed me staring at him with a dumbfounded expression.

"Those are wax," I informed him.

"So I noticed," he answered as if nothing was wrong and returned the mutilated and saliva-coated grape to the bowl. "You got your messager?"

"Yep," I replied and set it on the kitchen table. "You know how to use it?"

"I'm not a complete idiot," he returned. He pressed the record button at its edge.

I stood back and smiled an uncertain smile as it scanned me. "Hello, Uncle," I began. "I suspect you've received word from ASP security that I went missing, and perhaps even that I was shot. I'm here to tell you I'm all right. I'm safe and nothing's wrong. I'm here, at home, with the Commander."

The Commander suddenly stepped into view and waved his hand. "Hello, Uncle!" he shouted happily, and then said to me. "Oh, sorry." He quickly stepped away.

"That's the Commander," I said with a chuckle. "And no, don't worry. I didn't run off and join the Space Corps." I paused and looked away briefly. "We were . . . I was . . ."

I was reluctant to continue.

"I'm going on a trip with him," I stated with a forced confidence. "I want to see what's out there, Uncle. I hope you can understand. I know it's unexpected. I know it's something that I should have told you in person, but Servitude said you were harvesting, and, well, the Commander's all set on leaving as soon as possible, and—"

"Sure, blame me," interrupted the Commander.

I grinned insecurely. "That's a lame excuse, I know, but . . . I'll return soon, so it's not good-bye . . . See you, Uncle, and . . . please don't worry." I paused and looked toward the Commander. "I guess that's it, Commander."

He stopped the recording. "You ready?"

"Ready," I replied.

CLAIRE CARTER'S QUARTERS

I turned to look back. Sebastian watched glumly. He stopped at the base of the plateau and didn't want to move any closer to the gleaming ship that was the Dee-Dee. He gave a sulking whine and sat ever so nervously.

"One question," the Commander calmly said. "Are you sure you want to leave this place?"

I looked at him.

"Because when you leave this place and return, all that you know and see here will appear different. The journeys that lie ahead *will* change you."

I looked out over the golden field. It was beautiful beyond description. It was home. How could it ever appear different to me?

"Are you absolutely certain?" asked the Commander.

I looked back at him. "Of course," I returned, unbothered.

"All right then," he said. He touched my neck with a cylinder device. It gave a swishing sound accompanied by a severe pinch.

"Ouch!" I exclaimed. "What was that?"

"I injected you with microfortifiers. They'll protect you from astral contaminants and getting sick all over my clean floors."

"Thanks, I guess," I replied rather uncertainly while rubbing my neck.

"Let's go." He quickly continued toward the Dee-Dee.

I looked at the field and then down at Sebastian. "So long, Sebastian," I said, "I'll miss ya!" He gave a series of cries as if he knew I was leaving for longer than usual.

"I'll be okay, Sebastian!" I hollered. "Take care of Uncle for me!" As I stepped onto the ramp and into the Dee-Dee, he barked a reluctant good-bye.

"This is alpha hold!" announced the Commander as the ramp closed. I took one last glance at the golden field before the ramp obliterated the view. After walking across this vast room we entered through another door. "Omega hold!" he announced.

I hadn't noticed the detail on my earlier exit from these holds, but as I reentered them, I became more attentive. All this was to become my new home.

The next door with a triangular window opened, and we entered the hall leading toward the garden. The light within the Dee-Dee was now dim in comparison to before.

"It's becoming evening aboard the Dee-Dee. You'll become accustomed to this." He pointed to a door on the left and another to the right. "Guest quarters." He continued to another pair of doors before the garden. "My quarters," he said pointing to the door on the right. "Claire's quarters," he said solemnly, pointing to the door opposite. "Now your quarters."

He touched a shaded square beside the door. The door opened silently. I glanced inward. "I'll leave you to get settled," he said. "I'll show you the rest later."

I took a reluctant step in. "Um," I began as I turned to find the door had already closed. Whatever I needed to know would, for the time being, have to wait. The Commander seemed to be in a hurry to leave. Perhaps he didn't want to be located by some observation satellite or patrol craft and then confronted like we were at the ASP.

I continued my investigation of the room. It was much more spacious than the cramped shuttleport lodgings that I was used to, and obviously Claire had kept her quarters tidy. Everything had its place. A gilt wood X-frame cot, table, and shapely closet were located in the far right corner. To the immediate right was a polished white and metallic counter that served as a personal kitchen. Between the closet and counter was a doorway that led to a lavatory. For a ship so astral, it seemed strange to see all the conveniences were so Earthlike.

Directly in the center of the room was an elegant oval mahogany dining table with chairs at each end. A simplistic but fancily decorated pottery bowl sat in the middle. A large floral carpet covered the glimmering white floor.

On the opposite side of the room were wooden shelves that lined the entirety of the surrounding walls and reached from floor to ceiling. In the center of this area sat an ornately carved blackened oak desk and chair. Rams' heads garnished the corners of each with cloven hooves as feet. The furnishings were a great contrast to the otherwise polished white and cold metallic decor. This was where I would be living—utter royal luxury compared to what I was used to.

I set my duffel bag beside the closet and slowly walked toward the shelves. Books, jewel-encrusted rocks, brilliant crystals of varying colors, fossils, skulls and bones of unknown origin, and strange artifacts rested upon these shelves. They were breathtaking and left much to the imagination. Larger specimens sat on the floor in front and in available corners. They seemed to be all souvenirs of Claire's past travels.

Closer investigation revealed an interesting selection of small books, each with handscripted numbers on their spines.

These filled an entire shelf. I randomly pulled one down and opened it. The pages were dated. Careful entries followed; detailed drawings too. They appeared to be Claire's personal journals. I thought it amazing that she preferred antiquated handscript rather than a tablet. A tablet could hold whatever was scripted within and infinitely more. But there was something distinctly more personal about these handscripted books. It was the human touch. I thought it wrong to be perusing Claire's personal notes, even if she was no longer walking among us. It just didn't seem right. I carefully returned it to its place.

I was surprised to see that no pictures of family or friends were hung from the walls or present on any of the shelves to view—instead, only planetary and geologic maps and galactic star charts. Perhaps these had sufficed as family.

I sat on Claire's cot. It was mine now, but at that moment it seemed only right that I should look upon it as Claire's. She had spent time here, numerous cycles. It was eerie. I almost felt her presence . . . There was complete silence. It was so quiet I could hear my heart beating.

For no particular reason I happened to glance down and to the side. There looked to be a corner of a piece of pale pink paper sticking out from beneath her pillow. I pulled on it. It was tightly folded and attached to a messager disk. I looked at it for a time before unfolding it. It didn't seem right, but I did so anyway. There was antiquated handscript, the same as was within the journals.

Dear Starchaser,

That was me. *I'm the starchaser,* I excitedly thought to myself, although knowing it *could* mean anyone. I continued reading.

This note follows with what I understand to be a long tradition for us travelers, one which to the best of my knowledge the Commander knows nothing of. Unlike previous others, I leave you this messager. Activate it so we might meet more formally, and much will be revealed.

Claire Deborah Ellen Carter

I set the messager on the cot side table and activated it as her note instructed. A solid light image of an old woman flickered on. I didn't immediately recognize her but soon realized it was Claire Carter. She didn't look to be in failing health. She must have recorded it sometime before. The messager scanned me.

"Your name, please?" her soft voice asked politely.

"Bishop Hays," I replied. *Perhaps that wasn't enough,* I immediately thought. Claire had written her entire name. It was proper etiquette—antiquated, but proper. Perhaps that was what I should do. "Bishop Alexandrah Hays," I replied again.

"Greetings, Bishop Alexandrah Hays. I see that you have found my note tucked under my pillow. One day you may leave a message such as this for the next, but I pray it will be a long, long time away. Great journeys lay ahead of you with the Commander, my dear Bishop. The Commander does not choose his companions thoughtlessly. You possess something unique, something rare, whatever it may be. He is a man of great depth and knowledge and understanding. You will see much through his eyes, and he will see much through yours; this I know. And, yes, he is eccentric at times. Trust in the Commander, for he is a good man with a great heart, as you must already know. Undoubtedly you knew it immediately. Also, trust in the Divine, for there are things in this existence the sciences of man cannot explain and are meant to remain a mystery to us. Do not dwell so much on them; this I speak from experience.

"I depart this cosmic realm as it is to be, and I await the great awakening. Perhaps then we will meet, apart from this rather artificial method. For now, feel free to read my journals and use my belongings as they were your own; what was once mine is now yours, to do with as you wish. This messager contains all my thoughts and experiences. Consult me whenever you feel the need. I—or rather this artificial likeness of myself—will aid you to the best of *its* ability. Be strong, be well, and Godspeed, Bishop Alexandrah Hays.

"P.S. Take note of the sixth verse of King Dafydd's Warning. I feel it is near . . ."

Claire's message ended; her image disappeared. I blankly stared at the messager disk. Claire's message was spoken with great kindness and affection—except for her postscript, which was said with a distinct air of concern. King Dafydd's Warning had unarguable truth. There were "wars and whispers of wars" looming, but it was the "darkness of the expanse beyond" to what she was undoubtedly referring, and its meaning was left unknown to me as well as the brightest scholars.

I pondered what Claire had said. I pondered her invitation to consult her. There was so much to ask, where would I start? Then it came to me. Something *was* vexing me: the Commander's *name*. Surely she knew it after all that time being with him.

I activated the messager. It scanned me. The image of Claire reappeared.

"Question already, Bishop? My, you are a curious one," she said cheerfully. "You *burn* with question and *thirst* for answer. How can I help?"

"What is the Commander's name?" I asked, almost demanding to know.

Claire chuckled; she reminded me of myself. "Though I know it, it is not my place to reveal it." She smiled. "He will reveal it when it is time, Bishop; rest assured . . ." A moment later, Claire's image disappeared.

Disappointing, I thought. Suddenly the Commander's voice seemed to speak from nowhere.

"Bishop to the bridge."

This would be the beginning of my starchasing.

Exploration is a recipe of unknown destination.
It is part perseverance and part insanity.
I'm halfway there.

Deep Space Commodore Axel Linus Creering
(The Eccentric)
Loyal Space Corps
AM 7303

ENTHRALLED

11 October AM 7454

I had only been a few days traveling across the universe with the Commander, and every moment was a new and thrilling experience. I had visited the famous gardens of Carcos-Tyg, a planet famous for its thousands of waterfalls and tropical forests, and the colony of dendrologists that lived amongst the tallest towering trees. From there, we visited the ancient ruins of Sheffard, the first Milky Way colony, where was found great astral-terrestrial structures in the chilling grasslands of the moon. I then saw the Milky Way Galaxy from beyond its outermost dusty edges. The bright nucleus dazzled me for hours as we orbited around. Then we ventured to the outer rim of the Andromeda Galaxy to gaze upon the bloodred skies of Thort. This arid and harsh desert moon was home only to a colony of mining mechanicals.

I had also seen from orbit the Septenary Suns of Sequest, a secluded star system of seven suns that slowly danced around each other in perfect rhythmic harmony. All these wonders were places I had read about in the *Space Exploration Journals* and could now boast of having visited in person.

Other journeys were to places no other Earthling or colonist had ever seen—or, for that matter, heard of. There was the tiny nameless moon of ice where volcanic eruptions in the low gravity would return as frozen stones. Elsewhere, a gaseous planet glowed various colors; given its close proximity to its sun, the very surface of its exosphere would ignite and quickly burn out. A massive planet called Meed was encompassed in hundreds of uniform moons and resembled a beaded necklace. All sights were beyond my wildest imagination. Of all the places I set foot on, I made sure I took a souvenir: a rock, a twig, or a leaf, and I placed them on a shelf amongst Claire's past findings.

During these explorations, I had spent more time off the Dee-Dee than on. To return was simply to make a quick visit to the lavatory, drink some water, grab some tasteless vacuum-sealed food wafers from the kitchen, eat them, and sleep for a few hours, awaking to the Commander's voice announcing, "We're here"—and then explore someplace new.

To be able to travel virtually anywhere in an instant ultimately left one with greater time to explore. There was no time—or rather, I made no time—for a cleansing shower, combing my hair, or brushing my teeth. It was unlike me, but it just didn't seem important and didn't come to mind despite the scratching of my head. Although it was tiring, I was enjoying the fast pace immensely.

Now we were undertaking an extended journey of two days aboard the Dee-Dee, an unbelievable distance for any Earth ship to travel. I took this time aboard to study Claire's personal journals and read her detailed and unpublished studies of *her* travels to unheard-of worlds and encounters with various astrals. It didn't feel as invasive now that I had her permission. For those two days, with the added aid of her messager, I sat at her desk and soaked it all up like a sponge, but finally it was time to take a break. My neck was aching from reading for so long, and my eyes were weary.

I glanced across the room and noticed I hadn't unpacked my duffel bag. It still sat by the closet. I had become so enthralled with everything I'd left it there. I hadn't even changed from my shuttleport uniform, nor had I even cleaned it. And it was beginning to show.

I opened the bag and couldn't believe I had forgotten about the collage of pictures. I immediately set it on the X-frame table beside the cot and proceeded to dump out the crammed contents of the bag. Something tumbled on the floor and under the closet. I bent down to investigate.

It was the pink wrapped box, my mystery gift. In the excitement of the past days, it too was forgotten. I swiftly unwrapped and opened it. Within was a duty-recorder—a small device that when placed on one's temple could link with the optical and auditory senses and chronicle one's actions, much like a flight recorder. It was a device typically used by pilots and guard personnel.

A card was within, and immediately the mystery of who sent it was solved.

> *Hey Blondie-Blue,*
>> *Happy twenty-fourth!*
>> *I know I will have said I don't have a gift for you, but I'm not sure when this will reach you, or if it ever will. I sent it with some civilian friends I met—away from government eyes! That's why it should arrive at the farm. It's LSC property and they frown on it being given away. Have fun with it and record something amazing for me!*
>
>> *Love, C. A.*

"It's perfect, Charley," I whispered.

The Commander's voice called out, "We're here!"

Now was the perfect time to use it!

I opened the door and was about to run out. The Commander was standing there—completely unexpectedly. His hands were behind his back. His expression was serious.

"How long have you been wearing that?" he immediately asked with a low monotone voice.

I glanced down at myself, a little reluctant to reply. "Since I got here."

"Did you place it in the sterilizer?"

"No. I was just looking through my duffel bag for—"

"When did you wash last?"

"Earth."

"When?"

"The evening before we met."

"Right. Four days ago. Take a shower," the Commander said, handing me some clothes and a pair of boots with his right hand. "And put these on. That uniform of yours isn't going to hold up, and it's starting to smell. And if you're to accompany me on these journeys, you need some tools of your own—looks like you're staying." With his left hand he handed me a utility belt with several pouches. "This was Claire's. I'll be in alpha hold."

He was about to leave but added an additional order. "And use a dentite."

The Commander left. I grabbed some tossed undergarments from the cot and, as instructed, proceeded to take a wash. I entered the lavatory, stripped down, and hung my shuttleport uniform and days-old undergarments in the sterilizer. It began to hum instantly. All was similar to the shuttleport lodgings. The shower rained over me as I entered and stood in the center.

A dispenser contained an unscented green cleansing gel. My skin tingled as if it were gorging on my days of gathered filth. I hurried, wanting to waste no time to explore this new world. When finished I realized there was no towel to dry myself.

"Eyelids closed, please," a voice kindly and melodically resonated.

Tousling my hair and tickling my skin from head to toe, an encompassing ray swiftly pulled the water from my body and left me dry.

"Dehydroizing complete," it then confirmed, leaving me ready to get dressed. I did so quickly.

The clothes provided were similar to the Commander's and fit comfortably. I stepped out of the lavatory and looked in the closet mirror. *From one uniform to another,* I jokingly thought to myself. I fastened the utility belt around my waist. I was proud to wear it since it had belonged to someone famous whom I had admired. It was the finishing touch. It held much but remained relatively lightweight. It included all sorts of devices, each safely kept in a pouch. I took each one out and examined it: a palm-light, a compass, binoculars, vacuum containment vials, a multitool, microcellite injectors, stasis inducers, an autohydrating and purifying flask, condensed food tablets, an analyzer, a respirator, and extra storage pouches. I added the duty-recorder. Claire had used handscript in journals; I would use a duty-recorder.

One last thing came to mind. *"Use a dentite."*

I returned to the lavatory. A small canister sat by the fountain bowl. I opened it and looked in. Several dentites were limply resting within. I squeamishly placed my fingers in and pulled one of the gray, miniature, artificial, leechlike creatures out and placed it into my mouth. I kept my mouth closed as it crawled over the surface of my teeth and forced its way between them. It proceeded to move under my tongue and roof of my mouth and partway down my throat. It was then when I began to choke and coughed it into the fountain bowl. It wiggled for a moment and stopped. I picked it out and tossed it back into the canister.

"I prefer a brush," I uttered.

Done—I had wasted no time.

AN UNKNOWN REALM

I met the Commander in alpha hold. He looked at me up and down.

"That's better," he said. "Comfortable?"

"Yes," I answered.

Anticipation of the unknown was growing. Like many times during those first two days, the ramp opened like a doorway to a new world—which it was. There was always one thing that immediately struck me upon arriving on other worlds. When the ramp opened there was always a variant change of gravity. The gravity here, however, felt precisely equal to that on Earth. A moment later changes in temperature and smell would always present themselves. It was all part of the experience—tasting and feeling a new world. Exciting. Here, the temperature was cool, but there was no smell to speak of. This was truly unique.

As we stepped upon the surface of the planet, we slowly glanced around. Overall, the planet was dark, yet with a great many stars filling the sky, enough light was cast upon the ground to enable us to see the formation of the terrain around us. It was gray, jagged, and unforgiving.

I stared outward. Across half of the horizon a few purple-and-gray clouds stretched out and were touched with a glow of pale yellow highlights; the opposing half remained dark and almost sinister, yet at the same time strangely beautiful. The Dee-Dee's nose pointed toward this darkest horizon.

I became engrossed in the scenic view. To me it looked as though it was the end of a sunset or perhaps the beginning of a sunrise. Perhaps there was no sun at all. Maybe it was a special atmospheric phenomenon, unique to this planet.

While a cool breeze came upon us, a puzzled expression grew upon the Commander's face. "This isn't Foramjuruit," he frowned. "Why have we come here?"

I wasn't exactly sure if he was kidding or serious. I assumed the former. In my short time with him, I had often been victim to his unusual sense of humor.

"What do you mean this isn't Foramjuruit?" I asked with an amused chuckle.

"It isn't," he assured me, shaking his head as he walked out farther.

My amusement quickly melted away; the Commander was serious.

"You *have* been here before, haven't you?" I asked inquisitively.

The Commander looked up at the stars. "Never," he paused. "We're *way* off course."

I became concerned. "How far off course?"

"Oh, I'd say a billion lumen-spans . . . give or take a few million." He turned and smiled. "But not to worry," he added cheerfully as he proceeded ahead, "we might as well look around while we're here."

The Commander's smile was of some comfort to me. He made something that should be so serious seem so unimportant.

"How?" I asked as I trailed behind. "How can that be?"

"Well, sometimes the Dee-Dee has a mind of her own. She goes places with no explanation as to why. It's left to us to figure it out."

"You make it sound as though she's alive," I commented mockingly.

"Oh yes, she is," he expressed assuredly.

I was awestruck at the news. *A living ship? How could that be, exactly?*

The ramp rose and the Dee-Dee began to transform into a large boulder, cloaking itself in its surroundings. It was the perfect guise for such uncertain circumstances.

In the excitement, I almost forgot about documenting our arrival. I pulled the duty-recorder from the pouch on my belt and attached it to my temple. *"Ocular and auditory connections established,"* a voice from it spoke aloud. *"Auto-recording initiated."*

The Commander looked at me strangely. "A duty-recorder?"

"For posterity," I announced cheerfully.

He acknowledged this with a nod and a smile and continued ahead.

"This is Bishop Alexandrah Hays," I said quietly in an overly melodramatic tone, "on an unknown world in an unknown system, *billions* of lumen-spans from Earth." I paused and looked up and scanned the stars. "The Commander indicated we were way off our intended course for . . . *reasons unknown.* We're . . . taking a look around."

I then took Claire's analyzer from the pouch and turned it on. It took me a moment to figure how to use it, but it was rudimentary—point it to the desired target and the readings would automatically be displayed on a tiny panel-viewer.

While continuing over a rocky knoll and investigating various unique geological formations, I quickly took note of thousands of sparkling white crystals on an upright wedge of stone.

"Wow," I said as I rubbed my finger over one.

It perhaps wasn't the wisest choice, touching something astral-terrestrial. The Space Corps and Civil Sectors had certain protocols to follow regarding the exploration of a new world. Our very walking on the planet was against initial procedure. There might be some form of harmful contaminant, but this did not seem to bother the Commander, nor did it bother me. We were too enthused. Besides, the Commander had boosted me with microfortifiers, assuring my protection.

Another smaller crystal beside the one I was touching was loose. I aimed the analyzer at it. Numbers were fluctuating all over. I couldn't seem to get an accurate reading. This was a perfect opportunity to obtain a sample, I thought. I would examine it in greater detail later. I was careful not to touch it so as not to contaminate it. I took a vacuum containment vial from my belt and drew the crystal into it. A perfect sample.

"The place looks completely barren. Unless there's plant life somewhere, the oxygen we're breathing must be forming from a type of mineral degradation . . . these crystals, possibly." I studied the crystal encased in the containment vial.

The Commander raised an eyebrow. "Very good," he replied. "You know your quantum geophysics."

"A little," I replied. "There was a detailed article in the *Space Exploration Journal* regarding oxygen-producing crystals. It was from the lunar expedition on Mobius not long ago . . . It was really interesting." I returned the containment vial to my belt. "And thanks to Claire's journals."

"Ah, yes. The trip to Amaralah, probably," reminisced the Commander.

"That's the place," I said.

"Mm, one of our first adventures together," acknowledged the Commander, his attention focusing elsewhere. "Question is . . . what do they eat?"

"Who?" I queried.

"Exactly." The Commander pointed.

There, in the distance, a tall black spire could be seen silhouetted against the dark side of the horizon. Without further discussion, we began to approach this obvious landmark and minutes later came upon a plateau overlooking a vast stone city.

From this vantage point, the spire could now be put into perspective. It was situated on top of a dome, the dome atop a tower extending from among several closely packed structures on the far side of the city.

"Oh, wow," I whispered.

JOURNEY INTO DARKNESS

The Commander removed a set of small binoculars from his belt and peered through, scanning slowly across and up the various structures. The entire city was dark and seemed void of any form of life. He scanned it again to be sure. Still, there was nothing.

"Appears abandoned," the Commander uttered.

Instantly, I was enthralled with all manner of possibilities. *Just imagine,* I thought. *To partake in discovering some lost civilization in the universe!* This was something that I'd always dreamt of doing, and this was my opportunity. I'd be famous; my name would be forever noted among the famous discoverers in the *Space Exploration Journals.* Universities would teach these new discoveries. Long-distance starships would be constructed just for the purpose of traveling here.

The Commander returned the binoculars to his belt and continued toward a jagged flight of stone stairs. As we made our descent, we remained silent, matching the silence around us. The stairs took a sharp right turn and led us toward a darkened tunnel. Tiny refracting crystals adorned the entrance.

We paused, standing side by side, and for a moment peered cautiously in.

"Boo," the Commander said calmly.

I gave a startled jolt as his voice resonated. "Don't *do* that," I whispered with amusement.

The Commander chuckled under his breath as he removed a palm-light from his belt. "Anything could be down there," he uttered, making the onward journey sound more suspenseful than I needed to hear. He shone the light in, illuminating the passage before us. The adorning crystals reflected the light back.

Readings on the analyzer continued to fluctuate.

"Nothing's registering," I said.

"Put that thing away. You'll suck all the fun out of the experience. Use your own senses," said the Commander.

Without argument, I returned it to my belt. As we continued farther and farther down, the air became noticeably colder. I shivered and rubbed my arms; the Commander all the while remained unaffected, as if he were unaware of the chilling temperature.

When we had finally reached the end we exited onto a small open terrace. There were countless directions to go, and we wandered aimlessly from one curiosity to another. We entered strange open structures and passed through empty vaulted rooms and long, narrow passages and onto other open terraces. I continued for a ways on my own, and then something drew the Commander's attention.

"Ooh, look at this," I could hear him utter, but just barely. Hearing his fascination, I turned back and soon found him walking around a crystalline-decorated pedestal. His face was plastered with an expression of amazement. He shone his palm-light upward. My eyes followed the light, which illuminated a towering statue.

The statue was of a figure with its arms stretched outward; where there ought to have been hands, embellished sleeves draped down and cupped what looked to be a ball. The Commander focused his palm-light even higher upon the statue. The figure's head was shrouded in an exaggerated hood, its facial features nonexistent. Overall, its form appeared just as cold as the stone from which it was hewn.

My immediate impression was that the figure should have been holding a scythe, not a ball. It hardly looked playful. It looked like the grim reaper waiting for any unsuspecting fool who happened upon it.

As he drew the light down and onto a beveled plinth, he noticed a series of symbols carved into the stone—a sort of epigraph. He crouched before the statue's pedestal, brushed a fine layer of grit away, and examined the epigraph carefully. I was intrigued by his curiosity, but I wanted to make an equal or even grander discovery of my own.

Descending a series of winding stairs, through archways, past walls, and down a long, curving passage, I entered a vast courtyard paved with large squares of stone. Ahead was a building of massive proportions. I stopped and looked up at its outstanding structure. The building was so immense that the tall archways and gargantuan columns that encompassed it continued in either direction for almost as far as the eye could see. I felt miniscule before it.

"Commander—" I began to call in awe as I turned and realized he was no longer with me. I saw the beam from his palm-light waving in the air from behind several walls and terraces, a lengthy distance away. He was still enthralled with his own discovery. I refocused my attention on the building. I felt somewhat nervous continuing on my own, but the drive of a new discovery made me push on.

What is this building? I wondered. *What was its purpose to the civilization that constructed it? And what lay within?* These to me were all questions worth investigating.

In the distance I could see a series of stairs located between groupings of columns. As I approached, every step I took made a loud grinding crunch, and no matter how silent I attempted to be, the noise reverberated across the courtyard. I stopped and looked down. The stone squares that paved the courtyard had what seemed to be a fine covering of grit over them, making a silent trek virtually impossible.

I looked around for an unknown someone watching me as a cold gust of wind blew through my hair and stirred the grit over the courtyard. All *seemed* clear and safe to continue, albeit uncertain.

As I approached the building, I found crystals adorning the stairs and columns as moss would a stone or tree. I reached the crest of the stairs and stood before an open pair of stone doors. The doors were of a grand scale, some fifty cubits in height, if not higher. Whatever the true measure was, it exceeded all exaggeration.

I entered slowly and cautiously, the outside light doing little to illuminate what was beyond. In the distance I could see the outline of an archway; it appeared to glow softly against a surrounding pitch darkness, which presented itself as a welcoming invitation. Halfway there, the winds suddenly whistled through and made the doors groan upon their hinges, causing me to turn to look behind me.

The outdoor light that should have still been noticeable had vanished. It was as if a black fog was surrounding me. I removed the palm-light from my belt and shone it toward the doorway. Its brightest intensity did nothing to aid in locating it. The palm-light's beam seemed to be overcome by the darkness and completely disappeared. I turned it off and looked at my arm. I spread my fingers apart and turned over my hand. It was odd—there were no lights of any kind, yet I could see my own body clear as day; even the floor a short distance around me was visible, but beyond was total darkness.

In the opposite direction, the outline of the archway was still noticeable and in fact appeared much brighter. As I continued toward it, a strange murmur, accompanied by a faint series of clicks, occurred; ubiquitous whispers seemed to emanate from it. The sounds grew louder as I edged closer and closer—and then nothing. I stopped at the edge of the arch and peered around slowly.

There, not far away, with their backs turned, were three figures dressed in long dark cloaks. They stood by a wall and remained unaware of my presence; darkness filled the distance between us, as though *they* and *I* were on separate islands. The light that surrounded these beings and their position did little to reveal much of their appearance, except for their bald heads and bluish-gray skin. From what little I could see, they were surely astral-terrestrial.

A few additional clicks and murmurs occurred. The beings were speaking to one another—the ubiquitous whispers also continued, and strangely, in some inexplicable way, there seemed to be words I could understand. A cold, hair-raising shiver came over me. These strange astrals and their speech combined with the dark surroundings became unsettling; I began to wonder what had drawn me this far, what had caused me to press on alone. The eeriness of it all began to close in around me. Then, one of the astrals began to turn.

I hid around the corner and leaned against the wall. The astral had seen me. My heart was racing. I closed my eyes, took a deep, silent breath, and gathered my thoughts.

"What would the Commander do?" I uttered under my breath.

As if by some enchanted means, a sudden confidence came to me. I turned and looked again. To my relief, it had been a false alarm; the astral had turned to speak to another. It hadn't seen me; it wasn't after me; my imagination had run wild. I quickly retreated around the corner and rested my head against the wall. "I had better leave now before they do see me."

I hurried and quietly retraced my steps.

FIRST CONTACT

My calls suddenly broke the tranquility. "Commander! Commander!" I shouted. "Are you here?"

"Over here!" he replied, briefly shining the palm-light toward the sound of my voice. It was a welcome beacon.

In haste, I climbed over a nearby wall and landed clumsily on the ground. I looked up and found him standing in front of me. He stepped around, ignoring me, and fixed his attention on some symbols carved into the wall. The statue was ahead. The Commander hadn't traveled far.

"Amazing . . . simply amazing! Look at this place! It must be ancient!" he said excitedly. "It looks like it's some sort of . . . holy ground."

"Yeah, well maybe you should ask the astrals," I said with an exhausted uncertainty.

"*Astrals?*" the Commander queried, while turning and shining the light into my face. "What astrals? Where?"

I squinted and tried to block the light with my hand. The Commander, suddenly realizing he was blinding me, tilted the light down.

"That way." I pointed, opening my eyes wide and then closing them and pinching my eyelids. It took a few moments for my eyes to readjust from the unintentional assault of his bright light.

"What did they look like?" he quickly asked as he stepped toward me.

I shook my head. "I don't know, I couldn't tell. They had their backs turned."

"Let's go introduce ourselves," he blurted with certainty as he walked past me.

Just then, I glanced up. "They might not be friendly," I said, reflecting upon the statue.

"We won't know till we meet them, now, will we?!" he returned decisively.

"No," I admitted with reluctance.

As I began to follow, I suddenly remembered something. "They had bald heads!" I announced.

"Bald heads?" the Commander frowned. "How many?"

"Three."

"*Three heads?*" he questioned.

"*No*, three *astrals*," I corrected in a short fury of exasperation. "One head apiece!"

"Oh," he returned as though disappointed.

"And they were a strange bluish-gray."

He pondered slowly. "Bluish-gray astrals with bald heads. Hmm . . . interesting." He then began muttering to himself, trying to identify the astrals from my limited information. He began going through what seemed to be a mental checklist.

"It was strange," I declared.

"What was?"

"The building, inside. It was dark, but light at the same time—it . . . it was totally weird."

"If you're trying to scare me, it's not working!" the Commander hollered, reminding me of what I had said to him when he was failing to stifle my interest in exploration days before.

I couldn't help but grin in recollection.

As I once again ascended the stairs of the immense building, the Commander shone his palm-light up and observed its columns and arches. His light focused on an embossed circle above the door that was surrounded by stylized rays fanning away from it. I had neglected to take notice of it on my first visit.

"Looks like a place of worship," the Commander paused. "A temple, perhaps."

I remained without opinion as we entered, the Commander shining his light into the depths of the darkness. As it had with me, the light simply disappeared.

"How unusual," he said as he turned the palm-light off. He gazed around while reaching his hand out as though attempting to feel the darkness. "The light around us, it must generate from our own presence . . . like a visible aura."

"It's creepy," I whispered.

"It's wonderful," the Commander contradicted with a smile of amazement.

When we reached the glowing archway from where I had first spotted the astrals, we both looked around the corner. On the wall, an inset circle encompassed a dark blue light that was situated where the three astrals had stood. Like the archway, its illuminated presence was strangely unaffected by the darkness.

"They were right there," I whispered again.

The Commander immediately and unexpectedly walked toward it. I hesitated and then reluctantly followed. As I looked around, I quickly noticed that we had entered into the middle of a long corridor; in either direction, other inset circles encompassed in the same blue light were positioned at equal intervals on both sides of the corridor walls.

Upon investigating, the Commander noticed several embossed symbols surrounding the entire border of the circle. He then stared closely at a series of inscribed symbols of similar style located in the center of the inset. The inset appeared to be composed of extremely fine grains of soft, penetrable sand, and yet, as he tapped it, it was solid as stone.

"What is it?" I quietly asked.

"Don't know. What were they doing?"

"Just standing here, talking weirdly."

"Some of these symbols are the same as the ones on that statue's pedestal," he said as he ran his hand over them.

"They appear almost runic," I replied.

"Mm," the Commander agreed, "very interesting."

"What's it say?"

"Not sure. It's obviously a very ancient language … but nothing I recognize."

As he brushed his hand along the border, he touched one of the embossed symbols. Suddenly the symbols on the inset began to transform into another series; in surprise, I stepped back. Without hesitation, the Commander began walking toward another circle. I watched and then inquisitively followed.

Apart from differing symbols inscribed on the inset, this other circle, followed by the next and the next, were all exactly the same.

Soon, having reached another glowing archway, we looked around the corner. There, standing together at another circle, were the three astrals I had previously seen.

The Commander's expression of awe turned into a smile.

"Have you seen them before?" I whispered.

"No," he replied while stepping out from around the corner.

"What—what are you doing?" I anxiously whispered. "Commander!"

I watched the Commander walk casually toward the group of astrals like a child toward a new toy. He was much too trusting; there was no way of predicting these astrals' reaction to us—whether these unknown beings would be friend or foe. I stepped out and followed reluctantly. *We'll soon find out*, I thought.

"Greetings!" the Commander exclaimed loudly as he walked toward them.

The three astrals turned in unison, revealing their overall appearance. I found them frightful. Their faces were thin and gaunt, almost skeleton-like; they had what looked to be beak-like noses and large yellow eyes with vertical pupils within. A feathered fringe encompassed their ears, and their hands were composed of a thumb and two narrow fingers, all with short, curved, black talons. Curiously, they had no distinguishing characteristics of gender. *Perhaps*, I thought, *they are void of such differences.*

One of them held a staff with a crystal adorning the top, and emanated a wise and masterful persona as it stared at the Commander's hurried approach. The others too had wise personas about them, but they appeared in some mystical way to be the staff holder's disciples.

The Commander's approach soon revealed a contrast in height. They were exceptionally tall in comparison.

"I'm the Commander. This is Bishop Alexandrah Hays," he introduced us happily. "Who might you be?"

Without a word, the astrals again turned in unison and walked calmly away, ignoring the Commander's willingness to converse.

"Hey! Where are you going?!" he shouted. "Wait up a minute!"

The Commander followed as the astrals continued on and disappeared into an adjoining corridor. He then turned to me; I, in turn, shrugged my shoulders in bewilderment as to the unexpected reaction.

"How rude!" he exclaimed while looking to where the astrals had disappeared. Had he insulted these beings in some way? Was there some protocol of introduction unknown to him? What was the reason for their evasive behavior? Were they scared—frightened at *our* astral-terrestrial presence?

When the Commander and I reached the adjoining corridor the three astrals were nowhere to be seen, as if they had vanished from existence.

"Where'd they go?" I asked.

"Don't know," muttered the Commander. "They can't have gone far."

KOMORAH

The Commander and I continued cautiously through the corridor, uncertain as to where it might lead us. There were no illuminated inset circles, no glowing archways to provide any guidance—just our own auras that provided a limited path around us.

Progressing further into this near virtual void was not at all appealing to me; in fact, it was all that I could do to hold back from saying, "Let's turn around and leave—now." But if I did, what kind of adventurer would I be? After all, it *was* what exploring the unknown was all about.

As we continued for several paces, I wrinkled my nose slightly. *Something* was making my eyes water—*something* stunk. An acrid odor unlike anything I had ever encountered began to hover around us.

"What's that smell?" I asked as I held my hand under my nose.

The Commander took a deep sniff and then frowned. "Well, I know it's not you anymore," he muttered almost smartly. "Smells familiar," he continued in a reminiscent tone. "Very familiar."

The odor became progressively worse as we advanced, and although it was difficult to do so, we both focused our attention on the darkness ahead. Seemingly from nowhere, a short gust of wind blew through my hair and into my ear. The gust was unusually warm and moist in comparison to the chilling gusts outside, and the foul odor that was hovering around us swiftly became more intense, almost to the point of making me gag. The Commander too was immediately attentive to the sudden change.

"*Whew!* That's got a life of its own, that has!" he commented in a tone of disdainful disgust.

In a frantic attempt to gasp for fresh air, I swiftly turned and saw what the foul odor was. I felt the blood drain from my body. I tried to scream, but nothing came out but a breath. I took a step back as the scowling black eyes of a brown, boar-like creature with massive tusks stared down at me.

"C-commander," I managed to call out in a tiny voice.

The Commander casually turned to find the creature stepping forward. "Oh, hello!" he said, smiling without apprehension as I backed alongside and then behind him. "I know what you are! Could smell you a *mile away!*"

The creature stared into the Commander's eyes and gave a heavy exhale, causing the Commander's hair to move back and his eyelids to flicker in the foul breeze. The Commander held his position, though the smell was enough to incapacitate him. I held my hands over my nose and cringed.

"An Earthly *mint* perhaps?" the Commander obnoxiously asked the creature, blinking excessively.

The creature straightened up on its two stalky legs, revealing its true size. It was twice the Commander's height and at the shoulders was more than three times as wide. A pair of straps that crossed over its bare chest attached onto a belt from which a soiled loincloth draped and a large metal mace dangled. At quick glance, I noticed several scars covering its body. From continuous chafing, the head of the mace left a partially callused and oozing scar on the creature's right ankle. The pair of tusks that protruded from its lower jaw were severely yellowed and showed signs of heavy use; one extended past its nose, and the other was left jagged and considerably shorter as though broken from a past skirmish.

"My, my, you have been in the wars, haven't you?" the Commander said sympathetically.

The creature simply snorted as the Commander leaned toward me. "Remain calm; he's called a Komorah. They're only dangerous if provoked. Make eye contact with him, smile a lot," he whispered in a promising tone. "He'll like that."

"If you say so," I returned reluctantly.

As I forced a smile on my face, the Komorah shifted aside to investigate.

"Be nice and say hello," the Commander instructed.

I gave a reluctant "hello" as instructed. In return the Komorah gave a loud, snorting exhale. It then raised its arm and pointed down the hall with one of two clawlike fingers— toward the direction we had come.

"I think he wants us to leave."

"Maybe we should," I said nervously.

The Commander placed his arms behind his back and stood respectfully at attention. He wasn't going to move, no matter how intimidating the great giant was. "Tell your masters I request to convene under the code of the Zydok Agreement!" he stated firmly.

The Komorah stood tall, took half a step back, and gave a short rumbling growl, as if surprised by the request. It was apparent, despite the creature's appearance, that it had some form of intellectual understanding. It then pointed apprehensively in the opposite direction.

"Ah, that's better!" said the Commander happily. He then leaned toward me. "Best follow his finger. Don't want to be at the blunt end of his fist."

I silently and wholeheartedly agreed.

As the three of us continued for a short ways through the corridor, we were directed toward a small archway, visible from a greater distance by way of the giant's much larger aura.

The Commander turned. "In there?" he asked curiously.

The Komorah gave a snort of confirmation.

"Are you sure?" the Commander said hesitantly while nearing the arch and peering in. "It is rather dark."

Once again, the Komorah gave another snort and pointed, insisting that we proceed.

"Hello!" the Commander shouted apprehensively as he, and then I, entered. There was no response except for an echo from his voice. The echo was short, as if the area within the darkness was confined.

I queried nervously, "This . . . a room of some kind?"

"Sounds like it," returned the Commander. "A meeting room, perhaps."

The sound of grinding stone alerted us to turn back to discover a door sliding upward. Before we could react it closed with a gentle thud. For a moment we both stared blankly at the stone that now blocked our only apparent exit.

"Or perhaps not," I added.

"Well, perhaps not . . . but overall, I'd say this has gone quite well, really," he said optimistically, his voice deflecting eerily off the unseen walls. I glanced at him as if he were nothing more than a complete and total idiot. An awkward and lengthy silence fell upon both of us as we leaned against the door and stared into the darkness. I crossed my arms. The Commander followed suit.

"So," I said.

"So," returned the Commander calmly.

"Here we are, then," I said.

"Here we are," he agreed, nodding and smiling.

A moment later, I looked at him. "You didn't expect that, did you?" I queried with a forged kindness.

"No," he answered swiftly, while shaking his head. He then looked over at me. "Did you?"

I looked away and shook my head. "No. There wasn't time to think. It happened so . . . suddenly."

"It did, didn't it?" the Commander quickly agreed, almost patronizingly.

"Mm," I answered while nodding slightly.

"Mm," echoed the Commander, also nodding.

Again, I looked at him, this time puzzled. "How'd you know what that smelly creature was? That Camarah?"

"Komorah," the Commander corrected me. "I've dealt with their kind before."

"Oh," I replied. "And?"

"*Generally* they seek to serve the good, particularly the Old Guard."

"Old Guard? How do you mean?"

"That mace he has with him is a galanciad. Those who carry them are from the Old Guard, an honorable lineage of trusted Komorah from the time of the Royal Lords of Astraea."

"Oh . . . that's good, then," I replied with a tone of forced optimism.

"Although," the Commander suddenly continued as he stared thoughtfully into the darkness, "there was that time during the Putalopkey Scourge when an evil solar lord had a convocation of Komorah doing his evil bidding." He looked over at me and smiled. "But normally they're trustworthy."

"Oh," I replied, uncertain of what to make of his additional information. "That's good, then."

"I think so," he replied cheerfully and then sniffed with a dignified satisfaction.

Silence followed as we each stared solemnly into the darkness, awaiting the unknown.

Expect the unexpected.
But expect the unexpected
to bring forth as much displeasure
as joy.

Ackard the Wise Man
AM 7092

REALIZATION

The stone of our prison was unlike anything known. The analyzer couldn't identify it, nor did it determine any weak points in the room. I firmly held Claire's multitool crowbar between the door and wall and attempted to pry. With all my might, I heaved to no avail. The tip slipped out without leaving a mark.

Instead, maybe blunt force would work. I reset the multitool mode to sledgehammer, and the crowbar transformed into a long-handled hammer. Its weight was suddenly unbearable, but in my determination I swung it against the door anyway. A dull thud emanated. I struck it several times without making a mark. The astral stone was harder and more durable than anything I had ever encountered. In frustration I deactivated the multitool, returned it to my belt, and stared at the door.

I was hungry after my strenuous argument with the door. I took one of the condensed food tablets from a pouch and began to chew it. The Commander, meanwhile, was intently studying a pictograph spanning a wall. I pulled back my sleeve and looked at my time-keep. It had been well over an hour since the giant creature had imprisoned us, and the Commander seemed oblivious. I walked toward him and was about to speak when I suddenly noticed a glint in the corner of my eye. My aura had shone upon the edge of some obscure artifact. I stopped and took a moment to focus on what it might be before proceeding any further. Uncertain as to what exactly I was looking at, I slowly stepped closer.

It was a soft-white and rather odd-looking creation, somewhat reminiscent of some cubic style Old Earth sculpture. Infatuated by its smooth finish, I proceeded to touch it. As I did so, the room in its entirety suddenly came aglow in a warm parchment shade of yellow. For an instant, the change of light startled me and caused me to pull my hand away. The room quickly dimmed.

The Commander meanwhile had taken notice of my discovery. "Do that again!" he ordered without any regard for my startled state.

Like a drone sent on some fool's errand, I touched my fingertips against the sculpture without hesitation. Once again the room instantly came aglow.

"Interesting," the Commander uttered as he glanced up and around the room.

The light now revealed the room's octagonal shape and size, enabling the pictographs that covered the other walls to be visible as a whole.

"Stay there," he ordered in an almost inconsiderate tone as he turned his attention to the nearest pictograph.

I sat on a flattened surface protruding from the sculpture and quietly watched as though the Commander were a spider wandering aimlessly to and fro. The pictographs were strange. Each wall was different: one with a grid of ten squares and circles and three-dimensional shapes, each surrounded by runic symbols; another wall with a pair of figures and more beneath that and so on, all positioned as a pyramid; and another wall with patterns of clustered dots.

Despite my interest in astral-terrestrial archaeology, our surroundings were of little consequence to me. I had, at the moment, more pressing things on my mind than investigating the room's every artistic detail: What might these astrals have in store for us? How were we going to leave? And when? I wished I had brought Claire's messager with me. Perhaps she—or, rather, her scanned memories—would reveal some information.

"I wish Claire was here," I said, not realizing.

"Why?" asked the Commander.

"Because maybe she could help us."

"Impossible," returned the Commander.

"Why?" I asked.

"Because. She's dead," he answered bluntly.

"Yes, I know. But if she wasn't, I wish she were here."

"Then you wouldn't be," he answered, infuriatingly stating the obvious. "Besides, Claire's strongpoint was geology, not archaeology," finished the Commander, in an almost impatient tone.

A moment passed. It was becoming ridiculous, this waiting. I took another food tablet from my pouch and was just about to put it in my mouth.

"You know, if you keep eating those things they'll make you fat," said the Commander bluntly. It was as though he had eyes in the back of his head.

I looked at it. Just for spite I put it in my mouth. "At this rate, who'll notice?" I muttered.

"What's that?" he asked.

I avoided repeating my sarcasm and replaced my comment with another question. "Why don't you use your disruptor thingy?" I asked inquisitively.

"Why?" inquired the Commander calmly, as if everything was as it should be.

"To open the door," I snapped.

"Why would I want to open the door?"

I frowned. "So we can leave?"

"No. I want to talk with them—find out who they are. This is an ancient civilization. Think what we could learn!"

"How do you know they're even going to come back?" I asked as my eyes scanned the room. "They could just . . . leave us here." The thought of being left in the room brought a chill to me. I didn't relish the idea of becoming part of this ancient civilization and having some other inquisitor mull over my dry and dusty bones a hundred or a thousand cycles later.

"I requested a convening. Someone has to come," he replied in a confident tone. He then noticed an interesting image within a pictograph. At the center was a circle with several lines fanning out from it. It was surrounded by three beings loosely resembling the three astrals we had seen. The lines that fanned out from the center stretched across the wall and stopped at varying distances. The ends of the lines were surrounded by various arrangements of clustered dots. He looked closely at each cluster.

"Of course!" he suddenly exclaimed in a burst of excitement before stepping back and looking at the entirety of the wall. "What do those look like to you?"

I glanced and answered immediately what I thought was obvious. "Galaxies."

"That's right! I know some of these!" he exclaimed. "This isn't a temple or place of religious gathering. Not solely, anyway. This is a place of learning and study. A school! A library! A grand one!" He began to walk quickly along the walls, looking over the pictographs and pointing to the different scenes. "Theology, philosophy, science, mathematics, history, exploration, invention—that's what this is all about!" he exclaimed and then said with an infatuated calmness, "Those three astrals, they were obviously looking for something." He stared at the center of the pictograph and moved to the circle exuding the fanning lines. *"Ooh, yes*—that's it!" he exclaimed. "I should have recognized all of this sooner!"

"What?" I asked.

"The Paraxidiax Goram Thosit!"

"The what?"

"The Paraxidiax Goram Thosit!" he quickly repeated. "The astrals! They are all that we see in this room. They were thought to be a fable, a myth." He stood silent and looked at the entirety of the wall. He turned as his face went blank during a spell of momentary recollection. "Gosh, I remember stories of them as a child . . . They're real!" he said in disbelief. "And I think I know what they're looking for!"

"What?"

"They're searching for the Orb!"

"The Orb?" I asked, curious, shaking my head unknowingly.

"Like the one that statue was holding! It was said that the one who would possess the Orb would possess all the wisdom and secrets of the universe." The Commander paused and let the excitement of it all sink in.

I, on the other hand, wasn't so infatuated. Not that I wasn't intrigued by the Commander's revelation and his overall excitement, but the fact was, we were still sealed in the room, and nothing had been done to remedy the situation. It was beginning to appear as though the astrals were going to leave us here.

"Isn't it amazing," he stated calmly, "how history becomes a legend and over time turns to myth and is told as a children's fable."

I shook my head. "And this helps us now, *how*, exactly?" I asked as I pushed myself off the sculpture.

The light again faded into the once familiar darkness, breaking the Commander's spell of enthusiasm. He looked at me as I stared at him, waiting for a response.

"Oh. Oh, it—it doesn't," he answered while shaking his head.

"So how much longer are we going to wait?" I demanded acrimoniously.

"Mm . . . yes," he voiced with sincerity. "It has been awhile, hasn't it?"

"Maybe it would be a good time to open the door?" I suggested incisively.

"Very well," he announced agreeably while walking past me and toward the door. "So that multitool didn't help?" he asked.

"Obviously not," I replied. "That's why I'm still here."

"Right," he returned with a newfound seriousness and began investigating the intricate ornamentation around the door. Various carved symbols were incorporated within squares surrounding the door. As he touched one, it sunk inward with the sound of grinding stone. He pressed another above, followed by another below. If he was trying to open the door it wasn't working. He removed his disruptor from his belt and held it against a square. It gave a high-frequency pitch as he began gliding it over and around all of the squares. A fine dusting of silt started to fall from between them. He stopped.

"No, this isn't working," he muttered, returning the disruptor and removing another device from his belt.

"What's that?" I asked as I watched closely.

He pointed the device to the door and moved his thumb over a control. "An antigravity emitter. A flirtatious young Space Corps captain gave it me," he suddenly reminisced. "Not sure, but I think she wanted something in return . . ." He suddenly refocused his attention at the door. "With any luck, we should be able to force it open."

A distorting heat-like wave pulsed from the emitter. The Commander lowered it in an obvious effort to lower the door. The device whined and a mechanical buzz occurred as if it was straining to comply. The door wasn't opening. He moved his thumb upward, attempting to push open the door. Again the device whined, and still the door refused to budge.

"No, it's not working," grumbled the Commander. He then stopped and studied the ornamentation. He began gliding his hand over the symbols and erratically started pressing them.

The door still wasn't opening. He sighed and crouched beside it and rested his hand on his knee. He stared at the door and frowned.

"Oh," he uttered suddenly.

"What?"

"An ancient story goes that a Paraxidiax student would be guided into a room where they would undergo a lengthy period of intellectual reflection. They were required to study what was within the room, on the walls, and answer the proposed questions—presumably by touching various cartouches, such as these surrounding squares. When the final task was complete, the door would open, and they would be freed."

"Sounds almost cruel," I said.

"In a way," the Commander agreed. "But it stops the stupid idiots from roaming around."

He scanned the room, looking at the images. "It would help if I could read these walls . . . but maybe, just maybe, I can." He suddenly rushed toward the door and began pressing various squares around it.

A second later and without warning, the door suddenly began to lower.

"You got it, Commander! It's opening!" I stated excitedly.

"Wasn't me," he replied while stepping back with an almost permanent frown. "I wasn't finished."

PROPOSAL

I stepped closer to the Commander as we watched the door open. Before us stood the three tall astrals with the Komorah towering behind. The astral with the staff stood in front and entered. The two others followed. Their movement was eerily synchronized. The Komorah remained in the hall and watched closely over them. They were intimidating, to say the least.

The Commander smiled. "Oh, hello!" he expressed loudly and almost rudely. "We thought maybe you'd forgotten us, and—"

The astral holding the staff interrupted. I instantly held my hands to my ears as a strange sensation occurred in my head. As before, ubiquitous whispers seemed to be emerging from the astral's clicks and murmurs—I was beginning to understand them.

"What is this power you hold?" asked the astral. "You speak an unknown tongue, yet we comprehend you!"

"I hear the same, Commander," I declared nervously. "They speak strangely, but somehow I know what they're saying."

"Do not be alarmed," said the Commander as he raised his hand to the astral. "The power is that of my vessel."

"We detected no vessel," the astral returned.

"You wouldn't," replied the Commander. "It remains hidden by way of special design—disguised on the barren mount above this city."

"You requested a convening under the ancient code of Zydok," it then murmured.

"That's right."

"State your reason!"

"You ignored us. We simply wished to meet with you and hopefully exchange greetings, information, knowledge. We are explorers, peaceful travelers—"

"Then your request under the code is unwarranted. The code is strictly for matters of urgency, which yours is not! You are trespassers! Your presence here is not welcome!"

"We most humbly apologize for our intrusion," returned the Commander with concern. "It is not our intent to be disrespectful."

A second astral clicked and murmured suddenly. "You should have taken heed and left as the Komorah indicated. We cannot allow lenience!"

"Agreed!" the third astral murmured firmly. "They should not be trusted to leave. They must be calmed! It is required! They are on forbidden ground!"

"Judgment is passed!" spoke the first in a series of deep unsettling murmurs. "You will be calmed!"

Calmed? I thought. *Calmed* sounded like *killed*. The Komorah swung his head back and gave a shrieking cry. The astral lowered its staff toward the Commander.

"Wait!" exclaimed the Commander. "You're the Paraxidiax Goram Thosit, are you not?"

There was a pause. The Komorah suddenly snorted and became silent. The Commander had their attention.

"We are," the astral holding the staff answered. "How do you know of us?"

The tone of surprise within the astral's tongue of clicks and murmurs was faint but noticeable.

"You are known in stories throughout the universe," declared the Commander, stepping away. "Only by the images on these walls was I able to decipher who you are. You are believed by many to be only a myth."

"We have remained absent from the known universe for several millennia."

"If you are indeed the Paraxidiax, and the stories are true, then you're a peaceful people—a people who do no harm to others."

"We once were," stated the second astral.

"This way is no more!" added the third. "Dire events have forced us to be skeptical of those around us! We must not show mercy!"

"If I may, I would like to make a proposal for our freedom!" the Commander proclaimed.

"It is unlikely that any proposal will sway our judgment," the first astral retorted, as it lowered the staff to the Commander's chest.

"You can't kill us!" I screamed. "This isn't right!"

"So it has been decided. So it shall be done!"

"Hear me, Paraxidiax," the Commander said, "for my proposal shall have worthy result!"

"Then speak swiftly!" the astral with the staff commanded whilst glaring at the Commander. "Our time is precious; delay us no longer!"

"You're looking for something!" exclaimed the Commander, pointing his finger. "Something that should be here that isn't!" He ran over toward the cubic sculpture and jumped on top of it. The room came aglow. He pointed to the center of the pictograph with the circle and three figures that resembled the three astrals. "You're searching for the Orb! The Library of All!"

The astral holding the staff turned its head slightly to the left and then to the right, glancing at each of its brethren. It then glared at the Commander. "You know where the Orb is?"

"I do," the Commander said as he jumped off the sculpture and stood beside me. Once again the room fell dim.

"Then you will tell us," demanded the second.

"First you must rescind your judgment on us," returned the Commander firmly.

The astral pulled the staff away somewhat reluctantly. "We must hold council to discuss your proposal." It then stepped away. "Komorah, guard!" it instructed in a loud, short series of clicks.

They stepped out into the hall, leaving the Komorah to guard the door. The astral with the staff turned to its brethren. They began to whisper in their tongue of clicks and murmurs. I tried my best to listen but could hear nothing. I then looked at the Commander, who had his arms behind his back, patiently anticipating the outcome.

"So, you didn't tell me the Dee-Dee enters your head too," I commented uncertainly.

"Didn't I?" returned the Commander with a somewhat unconvincing attempt at sincerity.

"No," I replied while taking a second to peer around the Komorah for a better glimpse of the astrals.

"Oh, well, sure. Hang around the Dee-Dee long enough, and you'll learn to speak all kinds of astral-terrestrial languages by heart."

"How does that work, anyway?"

"Well, the Dee-Dee has the ability to create a universal understanding, if you will. Languages may be galaxies apart, but it's the commonality found between them that's the key."

"Then why can't the Dee-Dee enable us to read the runic symbols?"

"'Cause there's no soul behind a stone. Just 'cause someone carved a circle and called it a planet yesterday doesn't mean someone else'll know what it means today. It could be a moon, a star, a zero, a hole. Spoken language is different. There's consciousness behind it."

"Hm." I tried listening harder. "Too bad she couldn't make you hear better. What do you suppose they're saying?" I whispered, forcing another look around the Komorah.

"Don't know," the Commander replied, bobbing up and down on his toes. "But I'm sure we'll be the first to find out." He smiled.

I noticed his attempt to make light of the situation. His confidence assured me that all would be well. A second later the three astrals finished their council and returned into the room.

"Well, what have you decided?" asked the Commander.

"Our judgment stands," the astral holding the staff stated. "The knowledge will be exhumed from you by force!"

The Commander's face went blank.

"What? You can't!" I cried.

The astral passed its staff to the Komorah as the other two forcefully held the Commander's arms. It then placed its hands around the Commander's head. "You will speak!" it murmured loudly.

"Commander!" I cried out in despair.

The astral leaned forward, placed its forehead to his, and closed its eyes. It had no sooner done this when it suddenly opened its eyes and released the Commander. It took a frantic step back and gave a short series of unintelligible clicks and murmurs.

The others then released their hold. Together, the three astrals knelt and bowed their heads. The Komorah whined with uncertainty. I too was unsure of what to make of the sudden situation that was unfolding.

"Forgive us!" pleaded the astral suddenly. "Our judgment upon you is most unequivocally absolved!"

"Rise, Paraxidiax. Bow not in my presence," the Commander returned. "I am unworthy of this honor."

"Surely you are from a race of ethereal beings. I saw great light within you. You shone truth and honor greater than any others we have encountered or known."

"Rise and speak not of it again," said the Commander. "I am but a man, a simple traveler. I am the Commander; this is Bishop Alexandrah Hays of Earth. You may know of this realm as Aert."

"Indeed. Aert is the first world. It is indeed an honor to convene with one of the first world."

The three astrals stood yet still held their heads so as to not look upon us.

"Look upon us as equals, Paraxidiax," said the Commander. "Look upon us and tell us your names, should you have them."

They slowly looked up.

"I am Onu. I am Master," the astral introduced, "and these are my brethren ones."

"Sodu," the second said and bowed.

"Sertu," said the third and bowed.

"We are designated as Seekers of the Orb," Onu declared. "Our desperation to recover the Orb has required us to proceed without mercy. We have little time to delay."

"Then let us not delay any longer," returned the Commander. "I request your audience under the stars."

HAUNTINGS

The Paraxidiax Seekers walked in a triangular formation through the corridor, with Onu, the one with the staff, leading. The Commander and I followed alongside them, and the Komorah trailed closely behind.

"Tell us, Commander, how was our Orb vacated from these halls?" asked Onu.

"How exactly remains somewhat of a mystery. It *was* rumored that it had been discovered in a crashed Groke vessel over a cosmic century ago. Heard of them?" he queried.

"We have not," replied Onu. "However, identities change over the passage of time."

"Mm, yes," the Commander agreed, "they do. The Groke," the Commander continued, "are known to travel the expanse seeking to loot unsuspecting worlds or vessels. Cosmic pirates, you might say. Scavengers. Nasty people. Seeking anything of potential profit. Where they acquired it is pure speculation, but I strongly suspect it was from this very world. In any event, it found its way to a cosmic bazaar, where a longtime friend of mine acquired it. He's a collector, you see, of all things ancient and obscure from across the universe. He's more a curator, really; he holds most of his artifacts for all passing travelers to view."

"I see," replied Onu with concern.

"If I may ask," I delicately intervened, "why do you seek this Orb so urgently? Why's it so important?"

"Our world is currently under attack from a force unlike any we have ever encountered," answered Onu. "As we retain little knowledge of the tactics of war, our defensive strengths grow weak. The Orb will provide us with guidance."

"It will provide us with knowledge," Sodu added.

"It will provide us with the knowledge to destroy them," confessed Sertu bluntly.

"I recall a story that the Paraxidiax parted ways from the knowledge, that you left the Orb behind," said the Commander.

"Yes," agreed Onu reluctantly. "This is true."

"Why did your people leave the Orb behind? Why didn't you take it with you?" I asked in my typically curious manner.

"Although the Orb is very important to us, it is also very dangerous," informed Onu. "For many millennia our people traveled the expanse and gathered knowledge. We built this city of solitude to study the knowledge, its intricacies, and its unseen connections to other, greater powers. We found that we had learned *that* which was not to be known or discovered, not ours to be understood. After much deliberation, our scholars departed from this world. Visitation was strictly forbidden. To separate ourselves was to preserve our people from the potential dangers of all that had been gathered. To remain in constant presence with such knowledge would inevitably tempt one to use it indiscriminately, unwisely," Onu finished solemnly.

"However, three Grandmasters remained as guardians over the Orb," Sodu added. "Chosen for their pure virtue. But even for them it was important to remain in a state of induced solitude. If at any time our world required assistance, we would call upon the Grandmasters for guidance. They would awaken from their solitude and consult the Orb as to the resolution of the dilemma posed."

"Until now, our world has always remained in serenity and seldom has required assistance," stated Sertu. "Strangely, our requests for assistance from this world have gone unanswered, and this is the reason for our return."

"Upon our arrival here, we found the Grandmasters gone, the Orb missing, and no indication as to why," Onu expressed with concern.

"It is *most* puzzling," stated Sodu.

"It may be as you say—that these Groke beings are responsible for the fate of the Orb and the Grandmasters. We may never learn the true reason for their disappearance," Sertu commented ruefully.

"It matters not if we can see to its recovery," stated Onu.

"Who's trying to destroy you?" I asked.

"They call themselves Desolators," Onu answered.

The Commander's attention was immediately alerted. He suddenly halted. "Impossible!" he exclaimed with great fervor. "The Desolators are no more! They were swallowed into the holds of Abussos long ago! A dark star in the Megeddon nebula! I was there—I saw it happen! I made it happen!"

The mention of these Desolators struck a nerve deep down in the Commander's being. The Komorah roared loudly in concurrence with the Commander's discord. He outstretched his arms and held his head back, breaking into a shrieking whine.

Sertu raised a hand to the Komorah and quieted his overwhelming performance.

"On the contrary," stated Onu, continuing their journey through the corridor, "it is apparent that these Desolators live on."

"How could this be? How could this happen?"

"A cosmic quake was detected. Several rifts momentarily appeared outside our firmament. It was from these that they emerged."

"Tectonic rifts?" I questioned.

"Yes," returned the Commander.

"I've read about that. The Tecton field is energy that remains constant throughout the entire cosmos. A theory states that when a mass of energy is emitted it is instantaneously absorbed throughout the entire field, and if the emission is powerful enough, the energy may be released elsewhere by way of a rift."

"True," stated the Commander. "Anything caught in the surf of the event source can be absorbed into the Tecton field. Through that it can be used as a sort of gateway. And the more powerful the emission, the more distant the rift. Problem is, you could be tossed out anywhere—a very unpredictable, uncontrollable, and dangerous mode of travel."

"Indeed," agreed Onu.

"But to cause this, the output of energy would have had to be colossal—virtually immeasurable," continued the Commander. He pondered this as he shook his head in disbelief.

"What could be so powerful as to cause rifts in the Tecton field?" I asked.

"A succession of mass supernovae," answered Sodu.

"The obliteration of a galaxy," Sertu declared.

The Commander pondered these details ever so deeply. "Yes . . . yes, that could do it. But how? Where? There was nothing even remotely near Abussos."

"Unknown," stated Onu. "Perhaps it lay within the star. We have been too occupied with our own protection to go in search of these answers."

"Yes, and without the Orb, we will surely perish. Then it will not matter," Sodu stressed with a concerned murmur.

"And the Desolators will not cease with our world," Sertu declared.

"I know," agreed the Commander sharply. "They'll expand throughout the universe and destroy every living thing in their path."

"You can now understand our haste completely," asserted Onu.

"Yes," replied the Commander. "I can understand all too well. They once destroyed all that I knew."

A DISTANT ISLE

The Commander jogged down the stairs and into the courtyard. He looked up and rotated around, fixing his eyes upon a grouping of stars. He waited for everyone to gather closer, and then he pointed.

"There," he said with a great calmness. "Beyond that small cluster of stars, you'll find the Orb in a place called Dur-Cee, a planet and star that's its own system and its own galaxy."

The three Paraxidiax Seekers and the Komorah looked up with an expressionless reaction. I squinted. The grouping was barely noticeable. For a moment I tried to recall the star pattern but couldn't. Of course I couldn't, I quickly realized. I was viewing this starlit sky from a totally unknown and distant perspective. Earth and its many colonies, and the star charts I was familiar with, were far off in another direction. I was likely the only human to have ever viewed these stars from this perspective.

"We know of this place. It is an uninhabited isle, a paradise unto itself," clicked Onu.

"It *was* uninhabited," the Commander said with a smile. "Like identities, places too change over time. It's now a bustle of activity, the only stop between two distant megagalaxies."

"It is distant," commented Sodu.

"Very distant," agreed Sertu.

"If this is so," continued Onu with concern, "we may not be able to recover the Orb in sufficient time."

"But surely you can traverse these distances," returned the Commander. "The stories say that you traveled the stars without restraint."

"Yes, however, our vessel sustained irreparable damage from the Desolators upon leaving our world," replied Onu. "It has taken us many intervals to reach this destination, and it shall be many more to the destination you have indicated."

Though I had earlier feared them, I deeply pitied the astrals, and now I was greatly concerned with the apparent fate that threatened them. I looked at the Commander. "We *can* help them, can't we, Commander?" I appealed without really thinking ahead as to what this might entail if agreed upon. To me, it wasn't a choice worth debating. It was surely in our own best interest that everything possible be done to assist these beings. If these Desolators were indeed as ruthless and menacing as was indicated, then their threatening spread across the universe should be stopped as soon as possible. If the Paraxidiax had a way of ending the threat by use of this so-called Orb, we could at least quicken their journey toward its recovery.

The Commander smiled. "Of course," he declared as he turned to face the Paraxidiax. "I offer—" He paused as he glanced at me. "*We* offer our assistance freely. We shall take you to Dur and recover the Orb together. The Curator will be most excited to meet with you."

The three Seekers bowed in unison.

"And we, him," proclaimed Onu.

"Excellent!" announced the Commander while slapping and clasping his hands together in a joyous fervor of excitement. He walked swiftly away with a contented smile. "This way, everyone!"

I followed with anticipation as to where this next journey would lead us.

DEPARTURE

The Dee-Dee's cloak deactivated and the ramp lowered. As we walked up it and into the belly of the Dee-Dee, the Paraxidiax Seekers cast their eyes over everything. It was without doubt that the Commander's ship was far different from what they were accustomed to.

The Commander led the way through alpha and omega holds, past the quarters, and into the garden. The Seekers watched intently as the Commander stepped onto one of the elevats. They hesitantly followed. To observe their hesitation was rather amusing. Something the Commander and I took for granted was completely astral to these astral-terrestrials. There wasn't room for anyone else, especially not the Komorah. I stepped onto the other elevat. The Komorah appeared concerned as he watched his masters rise with the Commander. He quickly stepped on beside me; his smell was asphyxiating.

Upon reaching the second level and entering the bridge, the Commander immediately began running around the central console like a madman. The Seekers looked on with interest as he proceeded with his rampant calibrations over the console.

Onu and Sertu were soon attracted to the sparkling golden light of the Displacement Drive. They stepped closer to the golden sphere and stared into its depths. The Komorah as well stepped forward and peered into it, its black eyes seemingly melding with the golden illumination and white light that emanated from its core.

"Tell us, what is the purpose of this device?" asked Sertu.

"It makes you go really fast," I said with a smile. I glanced at the Commander, who was wearing a half grin.

"It is unlike anything we have ever encountered before," said Onu.

"Of course! It's one of a kind!" I voiced proudly, just as the Commander had with me when I had first seen it.

The Komorah stepped away and gave a deep but quiet groan while rubbing his eyes. He shook his head in discordance with the sphere's hypnotic capability. Sodu took his place.

I stepped close beside the Commander, who was intently studying an image of a planet and bluish star, both rotating over the console. I interrupted, whispering, "Commander?"

"Mm," he replied, looking back down at the console.

"I have a question."

"Mm, yes, you usually do. That's one thing I've noticed about you—always with a question. Hold your finger on that circle thingamy there." He pointed.

I looked down and placed my finger on the intended circle. The image instantly enlarged and focused on what looked to be an Earthlike planet. "What's the story on these . . . Desolators? Who or what exactly are they?"

I waited for a response. I could see the topic was a touchy one.

"They are all that is weak and evil within oneself," he quickly answered. "Long before the Great Peace on Earth, there existed a great evil—conquerors of worlds, giants of old, Emims or Zamzummims, as some once knew them, as well as a host of a great many other names . . . Followers of Apollyon . . . Before their disappearance from this universe, the Desolators were created by these mighty men—these giants—to spread throughout the expanse, eradicating worlds—civilizations, bringing desolation upon any they encountered . . ."

As the Commander spoke, the topic brewed anger. He began touching various shades on the console harder with each word. The Komorah snorted in accordance.

"Most of all, one must beware of their whispers— their illusions. Only the strong-minded can avoid their temptations."

"What kind of temptations?" I asked.

"The deepest kind," returned the Commander dimly. "Imagine all your deepest pleasures, all your joy and happiness, all your dreams being unveiled. Promises of greatness—*lies*— are made to sway your will to theirs. Exuberant temptations draw you in, feeding on your greed and lusts . . . If that doesn't work, then threats are made. Imagine your most foreboding desperations filling your heart and mind with complete and utter despair. Imagine all your fears, all your moments of pain and anguish, all your regrets, loathing and anger, hatred and negativity embracing your very being, your very soul—a swirl of emotions entangling one another— confusion attempting to break you and rule over you. *That* is a Desolator."

"Oh," I replied as I glanced blankly at the console and then back at the Commander. "You're saying they're deliriously evil, then?" It was a poor attempt at humor.

"Now you're getting it!" he bellowed with a smile. But his smile was but a mask to cover his true, previous expression.

"The Commander speaks truth," Onu stated while stepping away from the sphere with Sertu and approaching the console. "We have experienced these very emotions."

"And if you fall into them? If you don't—or can't—resist?" I asked.

"Then you are harvested," replied the Commander coldly.

"Harvested?" I retorted.

"Integrated into the collective horde. Spending eternity as a Desolator."

"And if you resist?"

"You're eradicated," he answered plainly.

I didn't have time to dwell on what this meant—the Commander suddenly slammed his fist on a shaded square. "There!" he exclaimed, startling me.

Sodu broke his attention from the Displacement Drive and looked over.

"How long do you estimate our journey to be?" Onu asked while approaching the Commander.

"Depends where we park ourselves," he answered quickly. "To the Curator's museum, a trek of a hundred paces, perhaps! To Dur," he said, smiling as he walked past the Seekers, "we're already there!"

"So soon?" questioned Sodu in astonishment.

"Oh yes. Blink of an eye!" replied the Commander as he stopped dead in his tracks, turned, and inquisitively noticed me standing at the console. I was still holding my finger on the circle. "Uh, *helloooo*, Bishop! What are you doing standing there like a pillar of salt?"

"Holding my finger on this thingamy, like you told me," I replied.

The Commander frowned. "Well, come on! We've long since done that!" he said as he turned around and left the bridge. "Hurry up! We don't have all century!"

I welcomed the words. Not only was my hand becoming cramped, but within the close quarters, the Komorah's stench was once again making me feel nauseated. I had to get fresh air.

DUR

An unusual sensation fell upon me as the Dee-Dee's ramp opened. I suddenly felt lighter—I had slightly more bounce in my step. The gravity on this world was slightly lighter than the others I had visited, which seemed wonderfully invigorating, and its scent was mildly sweet.

We stepped out onto a dry grassy field filled with an array of colorful flora. Surrounding us were many brightly painted windmills with massive cloth sails, indicating that we had arrived in some type of farming community. It was strange to see that on an astral world, the methods of milling were not any different than those of Earth. Beyond these colorful windmills were several rolling hills with small villages tucked in among them, and beyond those were jagged, snow-capped mountains. A low-positioned sun glaring from a pale blue sky cast distant shadows over the land. It was Cee—the life-giving light of Dur, the only planet, in the only star system of its own galaxy.

The weather was warm and pleasant, and the air clear and remarkably fresh on this lonely planet. I took a deep breath. In all, I found it was very comparable to my home in Antarctica.

It was a kind of home away from home, an Earth away from Earth—a very comfortable place to be, I thought to myself.

"Welcome to Dur!" the Commander announced. He looked around as if he was suddenly lost.

"What? We *are* on the right planet, aren't we?" I asked.

"Of *that* I am positively positive!" he answered with certainty. "But what I'm wondering is why we haven't come closer to the landing designation." He walked into the field. "The Dee-Dee can be so very vague sometimes," he said to himself as the Dee-Dee transformed into the likeness of one of the colorful windmills. "You're hiding? Why? It's Dur!" he exclaimed, as if a conversation with the Dee-Dee was usual. He stared silently. "Oh, I know. You want me to surprise everyone with new guests! Fair enough!"

As the Commander briskly led the way onward, we reached a narrow trail and followed it. Nearby, a wooden cart was left to the side with no sign of its owner. The Commander glanced at it, quickly taking notice of its contents. He then picked out an elongated red fruit and bit into it. He seemed at ease with his apparent thievery, as if he were entitled to certain liberties. Perhaps he was, I thought.

Farther along, the trail turned into a grove of purple-leafed trees. The branches spiraled upward and drooped over. Clusters of long brown seedpods hung from the ends, some dripping a sticky golden syrup. Some of these had shiny copper buckets hanging under the pods to collect the oozing syrup. A few were overflowing onto the ground.

The Commander tossed the core of his astral-terrestrial fruit into the trees and caught a falling drip of syrup on the end of his finger. "Strange. No one's been changing these pails for a while," he uttered in wonderment.

"What is that?" I asked.

"Tuktooke syrup," he replied, licking the syrup from his finger.

"Is it good?"

"Yeah. Better when rendered, but still good."

I caught some on my finger and tried it, and indeed, it tasted good. It was sweet and had a tingly bite to it. It was instantly addictive.

"It'll put hair on your chest," said the Commander.

I then hesitated to try anymore, wondering if his joke held a certain amount of truth. The last thing I wanted was to look like a miniature Komorah.

Meanwhile, the Komorah was having difficulty navigating the trail. The seedpods were sticking to his arms and back due to his size. When he moved one aside another would attach itself. He began snorting and whining in a fit of despair. It was most unbecoming for such a giant, battle-worn warrior.

I stopped to help. "Whoa, just stay still a moment," I instructed. One by one, I carefully pulled them off while continuing to urge him to remain still. "There, you're free," I said, chuckling, pulling the last one off just as he stepped into a large pool of the sticky syrup and let out a mournful groan. "Come on, you big baby," I joked.

At this point the Commander was a fair distance ahead and disappeared around another turn in the trail, followed closely by the three Seekers. The Komorah and I hurried after them. The winding trail left the grove and merged into a road, where the Seekers were patiently waiting for us.

The Commander continued between a row of dirty, weatherworn buildings and into the middle of an intersection. He hastily disappeared around the corner and a moment later briskly returned and disappeared behind the building opposite.

He then returned, stopped in the middle of the intersection, and rotated around, as though he were looking for something.

"Are you lost, Commander?" I shouted. "I think he's lost," I then mumbled.

"No! Definitely not lost!" he replied, still looking around.

"Why's it so quiet?" I shouted. "I thought you said it was a bustle of activity here!"

"That's just it! The place normally is! It's midday!"

We reached the Commander.

"What's the date?" he asked.

I looked at my time-keep. "Eleventh of October. Why?"

"No, no—the date here. Anybody know?" he asked, quickly glancing at each of us. "No, of course not." he said, answering his own question. "They could well be having a harvest celebration. If they are, that's where everyone'll be, and if so, the museum will be closed for the duration. We'll check with the village overseer. He's on the way, not far."

As we continued, the roads were eerily quiet, the stillness unnerving. We crossed other intersections and passed the doors of various buildings, expecting someone to notice and greet us, but there was no one.

Several minutes later we came to a wood-and-mud obelisk house quaintly nestled amongst an array of unusual-looking trees and shrubs. The Commander pushed open a pair of narrow doors. "Hello!" he shouted cheerfully as he entered a darkened room. "Overseer Pindal! It is I—the Commander! I bring guests from afar!"

I followed as the Seekers and Komorah remained outside.

"Odd," muttered the Commander. "There should be someone here. There's always someone here. Even during the harvest celebration there's someone here." He walked into another room.

I was uncertain of our invading presence. "Are you sure this Overseer won't mind us wandering through his house?" I asked precariously.

"No," replied the Commander confidently; his attention, however, dwelt elsewhere. "Villages on Dur hold an open-door custom."

"Then why do they have doors?" I whispered rhetorically.

"To keep the weather out," he replied.

Although the intrusion still seemed a touch strange, I continued looking around at the surrounding decor as the Commander ventured on.

Dark polished furniture and heavily bound ledgers strewn atop of them cluttered the entire house. Some were open, showing an ornate and complex form of handscript. Carpets with elaborate scrollwork and others with geometric designs hung from the walls.

"Pindal!" shouted the Commander. "Have I caught you resting on your duties again? Come on, wake up!" He walked up a ladder and onto a second floor. I heard his continued footsteps creaking overhead.

WARNING

A window in an out-of-the-way corner of the Overseer's house attracted my attention. It was positioned between two scarlet zigzag-patterned carpets. I bent over a table to look through it. It was a transparent mineral, a type of quartz. Its texture was rippled and distorted the vision. A murky film made it even more difficult to see through.

There was a garden with what looked to be small figures about half a cubit in height dotted amongst the plants. They looked like pixies—pointed hats, baggy clothes, wings . . . *Wings?* I wondered, smiling. No. They were more fairy than pixie. Or was there a difference? Then I suddenly discovered one of these figures was actually moving. In fact, they were all moving. They were converging before another, one dressed in shimmering emerald velveteen garb. I squinted. What *was* I looking at? I attempted to wipe the murky film from the window. While doing so, one of the figures noticed me and pointed. Suddenly another stepped from around the window ledge and looked at me. I bellowed in fright and stepped back, banging my head into a hanging lantern.

The little being in the window began waving its arms and yelling at me in some guttural tongue. I rubbed my head and stared at the being as it appeared to be saying something over and over again. It was a second later that the little being uttered an understandable word before jumping off the ledge.

Once again it was the mental connection with the Dee-Dee that enabled me to understand the astral language. Unfortunately, it was only the tail-end of the apparent sentence that was clear—a single word to be more precise. The word was *sergrot*, or *leave*, as the Dee-Dee translated it.

I again leaned toward the window and noticed the little being disappearing into the bushes beyond the garden. Several others followed.

"Commander!" I bellowed in awe. "Commander!" I bellowed again, this time more frantically.

"Hello," replied the Commander calmly.

I turned and was surprised to find him standing innocently behind me while stabilizing the still swaying lantern with his hand. It almost seemed that he had been standing behind me all the while.

"You'll never believe what I just saw!" I expressed in bewilderment. "Or maybe you will—I don't know. I saw— There was—there were—it was—"

"*Really?*" expressed the Commander with intense interest, as if my frantic and failing attempt at a description was actually understandable and normal.

"Pixies—no, fairies!" I blurted.

"*Oh!* Perinthians!" The Commander laughed. "Look like you and me, 'bout so high, dressed rather brightly, transparent wings?" he rambled quickly with an array of related hand gestures, and finished by waving his hands like wings.

"Yeah," I replied.

"You saw Perinthians," he said as he moved closer to the window and peered into the garden. "Planetary guardians of the expanse. You're lucky, not everyone sees them."

"One was yelling at me."

"Yelling?" he questioned. "What'd it say?"

"All I could make out was 'leave.'"

"Leave?" he questioned while stepping back. "Hmm, usually they're more friendly than that." He had a puzzled expression as he turned and walked away, suddenly uninterested. "Come on, the Overseer's obviously not in."

The Paraxidiax Seekers and Komorah were standing under a tree as the Commander and I stepped outside.

"The Overseer's not here!" informed the Commander. "He's probably at the harvest celebrations in Fairfield."

"Where's that?" I asked.

"On the other side of the village." He pointed. "That way."

Just then a speeding Perinthian flew toward us and circled around. It was a young female, beautiful and shapely with short golden hair and a dress to match. She took a swift look at each of us and then hovered in front of me. "You must leave this place," the little Perinthian began in her guttural tongue. "A great evil has come upon this world!"

"De geeven sine," spoke the Commander in the Perinthian's tongue. The Dee-Dee translated it as "What sort of evil?"

It was perhaps best that he speak to the Perinthian in her own language than to have the Dee-Dee invade her mind and cause her to understand. It might well frighten an already frightened and battered soul.

She flew toward the Commander and looked directly at him. "The worst, most terrible sort! Unlike any other!" she replied anxiously as a shrill clarion sounded. She looked in the clarion's apparent direction and flew swiftly toward it.

"Tektek! De sine Perinth!" shouted the Commander, which was understood as "Wait! What sort, Perinthian?"

The little Perinthian didn't reply. She simply darted into the nearby bushes.

"Strange," uttered the Commander. "I've never known them to be very excitable beings. One thing I do know is that they do have a tendency to embellish things a bit."

As we all stood in bewilderment, four glowing yellow disks emerged from behind the Overseer's house and darted into the sky.

"What on Earth are those?" I queried.

"They're the vessels of the Perinthians. And it's Dur."

"What?"

"We're on Dur. You said, 'what on Earth.' It should be 'what on Dur.'"

"Sorry," I reluctantly replied, puzzled that it mattered.

The Commander turned and ignored the departing disks and stood with concern. "It's likely another Critoriam raid. It *would* be reason enough that the Dee-Dee landed where she did and probably explains the lack of presence of everyone here. We'll have to be careful."

"Why, what do these Critoriams do?" I asked.

"They're raiders. Every twenty-one cycles or so, they come and take what they wish. Food, mainly. Strange thing is, if it is them, they're a little early. Their last raid was only sixteen cycles ago. Cosmic pickings must be slim for them."

"We must go to this place called Fairfield," clicked and murmured Onu. "We must see this Curator one, at once."

It was obvious to anyone that the Seekers were becoming impatient. They wanted results, and quickly. Even though their arrival to Dur had been instantaneous and the speed of the Commander's ship was of surprise to them—being apparently

quicker than their own ship even if it had not been damaged—
it did not give reason to delay. They were here now and for only
the one purpose: to recover their Orb.

"Yes, well, just hold onto your cloak tails there for a
moment," the Commander intervened. "If it is a Critoriam
raid we've ventured into, Fairfield's the last place we need to be
going right now, and the last place we'll find the Curator. Rest
assured he'll be at the museum. It's designated as a safe zone
for visitors during a raid."

The Commander hurried onward.

The universe may be big,
but enemies make it very, very small.

Galactic Admiral Cornelius Clarke
Loyal Space Corps
AM 7452

EVIL UNVEILED

Situated in the center of an immaculate island of rolling, greenish-blue lawns and scarlet-leafed trees and surrounded by a body of clear sparkling water was the museum. It was an interesting and rather picturesque structure. Its tan walls had several long oval windows that were bordered in a heavy white trim, creating a radiant contrast. The feat of engineering was remarkable.

Several balconies protruded from its walls and provided an infinite number of views for the wandering visitor. Slender towers rose from several areas, some connecting to each other by way of bridges and others with suspended stairways, giving it an overall look of a royal palace.

Among this display of complexity stood one massive tower above all others. It was much like the Antarctica Shuttleport hub. It rose from the very center of the structure and remained untouched by any connecting routes. It was crowned with a crystalline dome that glinted brilliantly in the rays of Cee.

The route to the museum from the village was another wonder of engineering achievements. A network of square-cut stone bridges created a seemingly endless maze around the entire island; groups of large trees that grew from the water and between the openings dotted the entire labyrinth and camouflaged much of it. If it were not for the Commander, getting lost would have been an easy reality. But then I noticed something. I noticed the Commander turning at every junction that had an obelisk-shaped cornerstone. If the obelisk was to the left, that was where we would turn. If it was to the right, then that direction was taken. If none were found, then straight ahead was the course until an obelisk stone was encountered. There seemed to be a method to the madness. In all, its creation was designed more for a whimsical meander than some cruel test of wits.

Among these furlongs of interconnected bridges, only one crossed onto the museum grounds. It was wider than any of the bridges that led to it and perhaps designed as such to universally say, "Welcome all! You have finally arrived!"

We neared the crossing. On approach, I curiously peered over the bridge wall and into the water. Although it was extremely deep, I could see straight down to the bottom—and to an array of aquatic life calmly swimming about. All defied familiarity.

The Commander stopped. "Wait," he said.

The Komorah gently touched my shoulder for me to stop.

"What's wrong?" I asked, breaking my attention from the water.

"Apart from there being no one here, no one's *here*. I mean, there's always people on the museum grounds during a raid."

"Perhaps they're inside."

"Perhaps," returned the Commander, unconvinced by the possibility.

The Komorah began sniffing loudly.

The Commander's eyes closely scanned a sidewalk surrounding the museum. "I don't feel good about this," he said while taking hold of his binoculars. He scanned the doors, the windows, the bridges, the stairs, and the many balconies.

Meanwhile, I looked at the water and trees and rolling hills. I turned and looked back at the labyrinth. Nothing was apparent to me, but then how would I know if anything was out of the ordinary? It was an astral world. I returned my attention to the museum grounds, but not before glancing at the Paraxidiax Seekers and their guardian.

The Komorah pitched his ears back and uttered a disconcerting whine. Like the Commander, he didn't feel good about the situation either. The Seekers were virtually impossible to read. Their facial expressions rarely changed, and when they did, it was too subtle to understand.

Over and over I carefully scanned the grounds. Suddenly, something emerged from a corner of the museum. It was too distant to make out clearly, but it appeared, strangely—dronelike. I was about to speak when the Commander suddenly put his hand over my mouth and pulled me down behind the wall. The Seekers and Komorah crouched alongside. A tree branch helped cover our position.

"Shush," ordered the Commander as he removed his hand from my mouth. "Pray it didn't see us."

"What? What is it?" I whispered anxiously.

"Desolators."

That word, that name, frightened me immensely. The Commander's earlier mention of their existence alone had been more than enough to cause concern, but to be in the vicinity of one struck a chilling blow beyond measure.

"That's why the Dee-Dee didn't land closer. She would have been detected if she had," mumbled the Commander as he leaned his head against the wall. "That's why there's no one in sight. They've all been eradicated—or worse."

"Harvested?" I queried.

"Harvested," he confirmed.

"There's no Critoriam raid, then?"

"No," he answered.

"What about the Curator? Your friend?" I asked as the thought of him suddenly came to mind.

"He'll be dead," he answered coldly.

I didn't know how to respond. "There's just one, though," I said, hoping it mattered, hoping that was all there were. But it was a meaningless comment and more of me just hoping than truly believing.

"Where there's one, there's others."

"What are we going to do?"

Something entered his mind. "There's fish in the water, trees standing, structures," he uttered as he glanced around bemused. "They're confused—"

"The Desolator comes this way," alerted Onu unexpectedly in a quiet series of clicks and murmurs.

"It's detected a disturbance," asserted the Commander.

"We must proceed," stated Onu.

The Commander looked at me. "You know how I once said it was dangerous?"

"Yeah," I replied.

"The horrific, evil, and demonic and all that?"

"Yeah."

"This is worse."

"I'm going with you," I said with confidence.

"It's too dangerous."

"I know it is. I don't care, remember?"

"Look, I can't expect you to partake in this. Go back to the Dee-Dee while there's still time. Follow the cornerstones. The route back will be safe if you stay low and hurry. If I don't return, she'll take you back home."

"No," I argued with certainty. "I'm not leaving." I pointed to my duty-recorder. "Posterity, remember?"

"Damn posterity!" he announced with a thundering whisper.

"The Desolator comes closer," murmured Onu.

The Commander looked over the wall and between the branches. He was not pleased with my decision, but he knew there was little point in arguing, and above all, there was little time. It wouldn't be long before the Desolator would be before us. He crouched back behind the wall and turned to me and pointed into my face. "Listen to me, Bishop Alexandrah Hays," he commanded firmly, making certain he had my absolute attention. "Listen not to their whispers no matter what they say, no matter what they offer, no matter what temptations they present. Focus *only* on what you know to be true. Got it?"

"Okay," I said compliantly and nodded.

"We must confront them now," said Onu impatiently.

"No. Wait. Direct assault is rarely favorable. We need a strategy, a tactic of war," said the Commander quickly, reminding them of their admitted weakness.

"What do you recommend?" asked Onu.

"There's one way inside without being seen, but once in, moving around in safety will be the problem. We need to split into two groups."

"A diversionary tactic?" queried Onu.

"Precisely." The Commander grinned slyly.

"I believe we can be of assistance in this venture," Onu declared. "You, Commander, know the Orb and the path to retrieve it. We will remain and attract their presence. But take the Komorah with you. He will be your protector and serve you well."

The Commander grinned even more slyly. "Just as I anticipated," he uttered.

"What about you?" I asked with great concern for the Seekers.

"We can entertain an abundant number for a time," assured Onu. "We can harness the ambient energy, and here there is much to source."

"Now is the time," stated Sodu.

And it was. The Desolator was almost at the bridge. If we delayed any longer, it would be too late to follow with our quick-made plan.

The Commander pointed to a massive tree. "Wait for us to reach the tree beyond that bend."

"As you desire," replied Onu.

"Be vigilant," said Sodu.

"Be stalwart," said Sertu.

"Always," returned the Commander as he departed. "Come on."

He led the Komorah and me back in the direction we came. When we reached the cover of the massive tree, the Seekers stood and proceeded calmly toward the crossing bridge.

I peered over the wall, along with the Commander and the Komorah, and through the thicket of branches. The Seekers turned the corner. The Desolator now had taken notice of them and was moving swiftly toward them. The Seekers stopped on the center of the bridge. The Komorah gave a short and ever-so-quiet whine, like a dog afraid of being left behind. The Seekers simply waited.

I stared in amazement as the Desolator came into full view, hovering closely over the ground. Several daunting black tentacles waved from the base of a blackened and gray conical body. Its body was covered with large scalelike armor. When before the Seekers, it slowed and began to walk elegantly toward them as a tarantula advancing cautiously before its prey.

I counted: one, two, three . . . six, seven . . . nine, ten, eleven—eleven tentacles in all. It was an odd number, but it was an odd entity. It was the large, circular crimson eyes that were the most unnerving, however. Three encompassed its conical form and a fourth was situated above. If not for the Seekers, it would have been entirely impossible to know exactly what it was focusing on.

The Desolator raised three of its tentacles and positioned them like snakes waiting to strike down their prey. Protective shutters on each sprung open and appeared as claws.

The Master Seeker, Onu, raised its staff before the Desolator. Sodu and Sertu outstretched their arms in a welcoming gesture while holding in each hand a small circular shield. The shields appeared vastly inadequate for any form of defense. In fact, I wondered what possible use they were against any enemy that would stand before them. But to my surprise a distorting wave was emitted from the shields, and as if from nowhere, a transparent sphere of energy encompassed the Desolator. With a swirling flicker of light and the crackling sound of an electrical surge, the Desolator momentarily screamed out as the sphere suddenly shrunk and disappeared. It was all within a second, from beginning to end, that the Desolator met its swift and calculated demise.

"Ooh, I like these guys," cheered the Commander in a sinister tone.

Three Desolators quickly emerged from the museum and were in fast advance toward the Seekers. They began dispersing white rays of energy from their tentacles, to no effect. The Seekers had surrounded themselves within an impenetrable energy barrier that was absorbing the rays. Brilliant flashes of light bounced from the barrier. The plan so far seemed to be working. It was drawing others out from suspected cover.

"This way," directed the Commander, satisfied with the skills of the Seekers. "The best way down is up. Come." He climbed over the bridge wall and into the tree, and along one of its massive limbs.

I took a careful last glance as several more Desolators were advancing. The Seekers were becoming increasingly outnumbered, but it didn't seem to matter. One by one the Desolators were encompassed and swiftly vanquished by the same sphere of energy that had silenced the first inquisitor. I was definitely in the heat of the moment now, and even if I wanted, there was no turning back.

As I ascended the tree after the Commander, the Komorah faithfully followed. We then jumped down onto a dotted path of partially submerged stepping-stones and under one of the bridges. As I traversed these stepping-stones, I wondered what had driven me to ignore the Commander's wish that I return to the Dee-Dee for my own safety. It must have been something larger—far larger than the impetus that in the beginning made me join the Commander. This was pushing me in a most unusual way, and I didn't exactly know how or why, only that it seemed important that I continue. I was surprising myself. I had always been attentive to my own safety, always assessing things before I acted, always questioning possible dangers when uncertain and shying away when the end result might be harmful.

"Thought to harm, halt to danger, save from hurt from an unknown stranger," as my uncle Augustus occasionally quoted. They were wise words, and I wasn't adhering to them. A strength was forming inside me—an overwhelming confidence I had otherwise never experienced. And it felt . . . good!

THE PASSAGE

Crossing from the cover of the bridge to the island, the Commander and I, with the Komorah close behind, made use of the numerous overhanging branches of the trees that lined the route. A few openings were present, but for the most part we were adequately concealed from view. Apart from the cover the trees provided, it was evident that the Commander knew exactly what to do to ensure our journey remain secret. He was very well versed in the masterful art of evading the Desolators' detection.

For one, the Commander was especially familiar with reading the actions of the aquatic life in the water around us. When the creatures darted from view, he recognized that as a sign that a Desolator was approaching. He would instantly seek better cover if required, or stop and remain motionless until the menace had passed. Only when the creatures reappeared did he signal that it was safe to continue. An additional assurance was holding his breath during the passing of a Desolator, something he very quickly instructed us all to do. In close proximity the subtle sound of inhaling and exhaling was detectable by these deadly entities.

Despite the occasional passing Desolator and the now silent and unseen battle that was raging between them and the Seekers, there was something almost tranquil about the setting under the trees. It was mainly the water that provided this feeling. Its ripples pulsed like comforting heartbeats, a rhythm of unending life. This illusion of tranquility, however, was suddenly interrupted when, to my shock and horror, I noticed that caught between some stones and floating face up was a dead Perinthian boy, perhaps no more than twelve cycles old in Earth measure. His body was limp and eerily moving with the calm ripples in the water.

"Commander," I called. I was about to continue but was at a total loss for words. I knelt down to touch the small body.

"Leave him," the Commander said and paused with a remorseful expression. "Just . . . leave him."

It seemed to me that the Commander had already taken notice and chose not to bring attention to the disturbingly grim picture—perhaps hoping that I would, by chance, be looking the other way when I passed by and not need to witness the horrible sight.

The Commander led us into an opening in the trees. It was a sure place for a passing Desolator to spot us. The Komorah watched nervously as the Commander hopped over the stepping-stones and moved toward a jagged granite cliff. A mass of thickly matted branches made it appear that it was the end of the trail. He then tossed himself into them and disappeared.

I leaped over as the Komorah took an easy step forward. Both of us faithfully followed and found ourselves in a hollow curtained by the branches. I looked around. The Commander was nowhere to be found. I barely had time to wonder where he could possibly have gone when a hand suddenly thrust from between the branches, grabbed me by the arm, and pulled me through. I was suddenly standing beside the Commander and in front of the jagged mouth of a cave-like passage.

"How did you know this was here?" I asked.

"I helped build it," replied the Commander.

Concerned for a moment that he had lost us, the Komorah barged his way through the branches, almost colliding with us. To his surprise and relief we were not far from his guard.

The Commander turned on his palm-light and started into the cave. It was dank and musty inside, the kind that would sting even the most seasoned adventurer's nose. The microfortifiers the Commander had injected me with were no doubt hard at work, counteracting any of the likely astral spores.

We continued for several paces when a small whimpering voice suddenly echoed. I could immediately understand the language being spoken—it was familiar. It was that of a Perinthian.

"Please. I implore thee. Do not hurt me," the voice cried. "Please allow me life. Allow me to live."

The Commander directed his light toward the voice and searched. *"Akor gartey. Defeegun tine orgurguron ye unteeg. Tar frengun unteeg,"* he spoke calmly, which meant "Be not afraid. We're not here to cause you harm. We're peaceful travelers."

"He speaks the truth," I blurted, not yet having the luxury of knowing the language long enough to speak it. "We mean you no harm. Please show yourself—there's no reason to be afraid."

There was a long pause.

"Your language is very unique and familiar to me," replied the voice. "I only know of one outsider who speaks it. Commander, is that you?"

"It is."

"Then in utmost respect I shall speak the language of yours," returned the small voice in that of Earth's singular tongue.

"To whom do I have the honor of addressing?" asked the Commander curiously.

"Beyruth. Son of King Nezebezekon."

"Prince!" the Commander uttered in surprise and bowed slightly. "It has been a long time."

The being came forth and hovered at eye level. It was indeed a Perinthian— a nimble young male. He was filthy and far from looking like a prince, and from what little light that was reflected from him, he seemed extremely pale.

"Indeed. I was but a child. It is good to set eyes on a familiar friend of the Realm of Perin. Who is the outspoken enchantress with you?"

"Bishop. Bishop Hays," I replied with some reluctance in regard to his flattery. "And this here's, uh, a Komorah," I said, somewhat unconvincingly. I wasn't entirely sure how to introduce the great giant that towered behind us. There had not been any name given other than that of its kind.

"It is worthy to make your acquaintances. Tell me—is it safe to leave this . . . this dark and unwelcoming place?"

"No," replied the Commander. "Danger is still present."

"By now, I fear, if my kind have not escaped, then they have been destroyed by these dastardly aggressors."

"I saw some of your kind earlier. One dressed in a brilliant robe. They left in a bright light," I said.

"Oh, it comforts me greatly to hear this," said Beyruth in relief. "The one whom you saw is my consort's father, a general of the Perinthian expeditionary army. I feared that he would not leave this place alive. I feared that all would perish trying to find me."

"Who's the one we saw in the water?" I asked. "He was . . . dead."

"Yes. My squire," he answered sadly. "He was struck by the lash of an evil one while attempting to save me. If I am ever to return to my realm, he will be remembered with honor."

"When did these aggressors arrive here?" asked the Commander.

"By this realm, two days ago," replied Beyruth.

"About how many?"

"A hundred—maybe two." The Perinthian shook his head. "I cannot say with certainty. Without warning a great burning chariot came from the heavens and crashed into the mountains to the north. From it burst these hordes of evil, like a flood on the plains of Rookery. Without mercy they began their rampage, playing tricks on the mind."

"Sounds like a Centagon."

"A what?" I questioned.

"A kind of Desolator troop ship. We must continue," stated the Commander as he shone his light forward and proceeded. "I don't know how many the Seekers can hold off."

"To where are you going?" asked Beyruth anxiously.

"Deeper," replied the Commander.

"Of all places, what brings you here?" he asked.

"The Orb," I replied.

"The Orb?" questioned Beyruth curiously. "The Library of All?"

"The same," replied the Commander.

"The Curator possesses such a known artifact, of course, but it is a myth!" exclaimed Beyruth in disbelief.

"It's not," replied the Commander as he shone his light ahead. "On the contrary, it is very real. We aid those to whom it belongs."

"Their realm is under attack by the Desolators, these evil ones, as you call them," I added. "They seek the Orb for the knowledge it contains to stop them."

"Amazing!" announced Beyruth.

The Commander shoved aside a tangle of dripping roots covering a rusted iron door. "This is it," he uttered. He pulled on the door's handle, but it wouldn't budge. He stared at the top and then the bottom and pulled again. "It's rusted itself shut!" he exclaimed. "We'll have to force it open." He reached for his antigravity emitter.

The Komorah grunted.

The Commander looked back at him. "Go ahead. Make yourself useful," he said. "But be quiet about it."

The Komorah reached between the Commander and me and pulled on the handle. With a short dull grind the door slowly opened with ease.

"Thank you," said the Commander, smiling, as I covered my nose.

Between the dank cave and smell of the Komorah in the close quarters, I involuntarily gagged.

"Shush," the Commander said without care to my condition. "Last thing we need is to bring attention to ourselves." He placed his hand on the door and pushed it farther open, creating an unexpected rusty, deafening screech—the kind of high-pitched, gut-twisting noise that was beyond any other and in its intensity could, without argument, raise the dead across the total expanse of the universe and its unknown galaxies.

I cringed; the Komorah's ears pitched back, and our newfound friend, Beyruth, disappeared, only to perk up from behind a thick protruding root a moment later.

"We're done for," whimpered Beyruth.

It was at this moment that the waking of the dead from across the expanse was of little worry. In fact, it was of no worry whatsoever. It was rather the occupying Desolators of this realm that may have become aware of the noise and its origin that was of paramount concern.

"I s'pose we're in one of those real sleks now?" I whispered sharply.

The Commander raised an eyebrow and remained silent, perhaps to avoid any additional embarrassment in an attempt to make an excuse in his own defense or to apologize. To do so would be pointless anyway. The deed was irreversibly done.

He proceeded first through the door.

AN ODIOUS DISPLAY

We cautiously entered into a room. It was overflowing with stacked metallic crates, some with scrolling astral script on them. Though the room was about as dark as the passage, it was at least dry and not as musty in comparison.

Uncertain as to what we might encounter, the Commander turned off his palm-light. He looked through a narrow opening between the piled crates where a glimmer of light was filtering through. There were no Desolators waiting to swarm in on us. They had obviously not heard the wretched squeak of the door, for if they had, they'd surely be waiting for us. It seemed safe—for the moment, anyway, until the Commander, who was in the midst of reattaching the palm-light to his belt, suddenly dropped it. Everyone's heart sank as it clattered loudly on the floor. "Oops," he said as he leaned over and picked it up. He ignored his clumsiness as if it didn't matter and proceeded around the crates and into the room where the light was coming from.

The room was massive and extremely well lit. Incandescent rings that hovered below the ceiling were intense but not blinding. A strange phenomenon, I thought, as I stared up at them without squinting.

We passed several disorganized displays of obscure astral-terrestrial sculptures and paintings. The bent rods and twisted glasslike spikes of one creation seemed to imply that its design was of some exotic tree. Another work consisted of a three-dimensional painting reminiscent of some salvaged Old Earth Picasso. Other great works dotted the room, many piled precariously into one massive collage. It didn't look much different than an Earthly museum except, of course, for the sheer obscurity of many of the items.

As we entered another room we were met with cluttered displays of astral-terrestrial armor and weapons, both primitive and advanced. There was the easily identifiable sword and spear and objects that looked like distributors—the kind that would undoubtedly vaporize a person in an instant. But among these identifiable tools of warfare were those that, because of their unusual designs, remained completely mysterious as to their use.

A giant suit of armor embellished with an array of brilliant studs stood righteously, as if keeping watch over the treasures. Its stature was grand and was higher than even the Komorah could ever hope to reach; it must have been worn by some great and perhaps even extinct beast—an Emim or Zamzummim, I considered, one of those evil giants of old the Commander had spoken of.

Farther on, a strange, open-seated chariot affixed with what appeared to be some form of energy cannons and a pair of long birdlike legs appeared to guard the passage into the next room, giving the uncomfortable feeling that it could come to life at any moment.

As we ventured past this motionless sentinel and into the next room, we found that, like the other rooms, it too was overflowing with disorganized displays of artifacts from afar.

In this room were various technologies, large and small, from throughout the ages. Some were present in their entirety, and others were fragments of a time long since passed.

Immediately my attention was drawn to something hanging high upon a wall. It was a large, burnished sheet of tiled alloy with a black abbreviation stenciled across it. It was a very familiar abbreviation. It was the type I had seen in antiquated volumes of the *Space Exploration Journal*, and not too different from the type I had seen at the Antarctica Shuttleport. In old style lettering, the abbreviation was *L.S.C.*

Could it be? Could it really be from Earth? Or was it just some odd coincidence? Then, underneath, I noticed amongst the burnished residue were the very words to confirm it: *Terra Nova.*

"Wow," I whispered, virtually only to the satisfaction of my own ears. "The *LSC Terra Nova*. The first deep-space ship destined to find a new Earth. It was lost over three hundred cycles ago."

I thought it amazing that a fragment such as this could find its way here billions upon billions, if not trillions, of lumen-spans away. How had it come to be here? What series of events had led to it being hung on this astral-terrestrial wall?

Whatever the answer, this place was heaven—a wealth of astral artifacts bursting at the seams. It was what any astral-terrestrial archaeologist or scientist would revel in. It was sheer bliss—sheer heaven . . . *In hell*, I then thought, as I reflected on the reason for us being here, the Desolators that were gathering around the three Paraxidiax Seekers, and the small dead Perinthian floating in the water. It was not a moment to be reveling at all.

Clack. Clack. Clack. Whirrrrr. A series of sharp sounds repeated as we entered a great room, a room that would feed fear into the strongest-hearted and most callused of souls. I gazed slowly at hundreds of heads that rested on saucer-like plinths, heads not of animals, but of higher life forms. Most were remarkably human in appearance and others defiant of any accurate comparison or description. Was this some odious display of astral-terrestrial taxidermy?

I looked at the Commander. He had an expression of horrid disgust and anger. It was obvious that this was no display created by his friend, the Curator. We walked past, staring silently until I found the nerve to speak.

"Commander, what . . . is this?" I asked.

"The harvested," replied the Commander angrily.

As I looked more intently, I could see that the saucers the heads were placed on were in various stages of development and, even before my eyes, were slowly constructing themselves. Their growth was an astounding mix of flesh and machine. The sounds we heard were coming from a small black pyramid and looked to be a form of life support machine that sustained the harvested during their transformations into Desolators.

"It's terrible," I said with difficulty.

"It is so," agreed Beyruth timidly.

Unexpectedly, one of the heads came to life. An umber-skinned face with strange white barnacles opened its spectacular pale blue eyes and looked upon us. I gasped. The being's mouth jerked open and closed and began contorting its jaw in a useless and desperate attempt to speak—its vocal cords having been severed. Short stubbed tentacles waved frantically as if having a tantrum. The Commander swiftly grabbed hold and pulled a handful of fibrous threads from the base of the saucer. The being's eyelids flickered, and its eyes rolled to the side and then fell expressionless and dead.

"You've killed it," I said in an awestruck tone.

"It was already dead," growled the Commander. He then pulled the disruptor from his belt. "What it was was a Desolator attempting to alert the parent horde."

"What are you doing?" I asked.

"Stopping this," he replied while holding up the disruptor. The familiar frequency from it resonated as he motioned it slowly across the room.

We all turned and watched as the faces of the many astrals contorted uncontrollably. The clacks and whirs from the pyramid machine ceased. The heads went lifeless. Not a second of silence later a distant scream alerted our attention, now noticeable after the complete silencing of the machine. We hastened down a corridor in the general direction of the troubled cry and paused at the base of a grand spiral staircase. There were several directions that could have been taken, but another scream directed us upward.

When you feel as though the universe is closing in on you,
it probably is.

Commander Athere Seamus Dandedule
Loyal Space Corps
AM 7404

"MY FRIEND"

We had climbed four floors when another cry echoed. The Commander fixed his eyes on a room directly ahead and moved toward it. He had a strained look deeply entrenched on his face. We peered around the entry to find the tentacles of a Desolator delicately waving about, as if it were performing several microscopic procedures. As the tentacles suddenly jolted in unison, a scream of pure agony rang out.

An expression of raging anger immediately grew on the Commander's face as he clenched his teeth, turned to the Komorah, and whispered heavily. "Do what you do, Komorah, and do not be gentle."

This proposed assault on the Desolator had to be quick and successful so as not to alert the others and had to be done without being discovered. However, with the Desolator's crimson eyes covering all directions and the circumference of its tentacles in close proximity, it seemed nearly impossible.

The Komorah ducked under the doorway with his mace held ready. As expected, the Desolator took notice of the giant and froze, evidently taking a second to assess the situation. Taking advantage of its hesitation and leaving no time for the

Desolator to react, the Komorah swung a sudden downward blow over the Desolator's topmost eye, instantly crushing the seemingly impervious armor and causing a translucent red liquid within to squirt upward. With another swing he then bashed it aside, sending it across the room and through several displays. He gave a snort and backed away, leaving the area clear for the Commander and myself to enter. Beyruth trailed nervously behind.

My eyes were immediately drawn to an astral with iridescent purple skin and long, silver hair that framed his long narrow face. His four arms and pair of legs were outstretched, like the Old Earth depiction of da Vinci's *Vitruvian Man*, his hands and feet fused to a white seven-armed crucifix that hovered motionless on an angle. On closer inspection, I saw that several long fine needles protruded from his chest and head. Wounds where others had pierced him riddled his body. They had obviously been embedded deeply and were quite blatantly the cause of his agony.

Beyruth flew around the astral's head and hovered alongside. "He does not appear long for this realm," he uttered mournfully.

"Komorah, secure the entry," the Commander instructed.

The Komorah swiftly complied.

"How do we remove him?" I asked as I looked at the astral's whitening wrists.

"We can't," replied the Commander as he slowly approached.

"This is a septicrux," added Beyruth. "It will meld with his entire body in a short time. It cannot be reversed."

"It looks as though the Desolator was delaying the amalgamation—trying to keep him alive," said the Commander.

"Who is he?" I asked.

"He's the Curator . . . my friend," answered the Commander. "Pylun," he called to the astral.

The astral turned his head and stared blankly at the Commander and suddenly began to gently laugh. "Commander . . . is that you? Or do my dying eyes deceive me?" he asked in disbelief.

To my surprise there was no need for the Dee-Dee's translating capabilities. The Commander's friend spoke in the same language, as if Earth's singular language was somehow universal.

"It is, old friend," replied the Commander in a comforting tone, smiling forcefully.

"And where is Miss Carter?" asked the Curator eagerly.

"She has passed. Several days ago."

"Oh," sighed the Curator, "I am sorry, Commander. I am so sorry to hear of it."

"It was her time."

"Yes . . . yes," the Curator agreed.

"This is Bishop Alexandrah Hays of Earth."

The Curator made an explicit point of looking at me. His eyes locked onto mine. They were very penetrating but not intimidating or invasive. They were kind and caring eyes.

"From the first world, as Claire Deborah-Ellen Carter was. A strong name. A beautiful name," he said. "A young spark of light you are, child. Yes, a young spark of light. I can see it immediately." He then looked at the Commander keenly. "You always come at the most unexpected times," he said as he burst into a fit of coughing.

"Yes, I do," the Commander agreed, looking at his friend sprawled out. "I only wish I had arrived sooner."

"I fear there would have been little you could have done. The Desolators came like a swarm. They came during the start of the harvest festivities . . ." A faint smile formed on the Curator's face as he paused. A happy thought had come to his mind. "It was to have been a momentous event this time around. Erok had grown the most amazing sherip—One for all to admire." He then broke into tears. "She is now gone, her life extinguished by these Desolators. Oh, so dear to my heart she was."

"And mine," admitted the Commander solemnly. "I saw her among the harvested."

"I pray you ended it swiftly?"

"I did."

"How have they returned, Commander? Was it not long ago that we saw them vanquished into the holds of Abussos? Were some overlooked in some corner of this universe?"

"I do not believe so. They apparently came from Tectonic rifts."

"Then they have escaped from the grasp of Abussos?" asked the Curator.

"It appears so."

"Something powerful has occurred, then, Commander. Something terrible and terrifying."

"I know," the Commander replied. He looked again at his friend sprawled out and eyed the needles protruding from his body and his limbs melding with the septicrux. The meld had by now quickly advanced to his knees and elbows. "Why have they done this to you, my dear friend?" he asked glumly. "This is not the norm of a Desolator."

"I placed myself on the septicrux, Commander."

"But why?"

"I killed many Desolators on their arrival, as well as many who were about to be harvested—just as you and I had done in those final moments at Megeddon. Curiously, the Desolators ceased defending themselves against me, but still I killed them, and still they came. For me. I killed them until the weapon

I had could be used no more. As you know, my will is too strong for their whispers, so they cannot harvest me and obtain my knowledge. A Desolator that cannot harvest you, but will not eradicate you, can only mean one other possibility, and so I ran here. But they intervened before the septicrux could consume me. And I was right. They believe I am too valuable to eradicate. They ask things I cannot answer, and so they prolong my life and torture me. I cannot tell them what I do not know. So confused they are without their Tribune."

"It is as I thought, then; they're without a leader." The Commander closed his eyes and lowered his head. "My dear friend," he said with great remorse, clenching his fists by his sides. "It pains me to see you in such . . ." He couldn't find the words to continue, or at least he could not speak them.

Beyruth tearfully backed away, unable to look upon the horrid sight any longer. He picked up a small object from a shelf and angrily threw it at the crushed Desolator.

"You need not concern yourself, Commander. It is to be," replied the Curator. "We must speak of what reason brings you here now. I know you too well. You rarely come for no reason, and never with more than one companion."

"We seek the Orb, Pylun."

The Curator laughed and then broke into an uncontrollable, gagging cough. The Commander touched the Curator's shoulder and waited for him to stop.

"How fate intertwines us all," the Curator marveled. "These Desolators wish for me to tell them how to use it. They want me to reveal its secrets. It is why they torture me thus. They believe I know, but I do not. I . . . do not," he said as he broke into another raging cough. When he stopped, he paused and looked into the Commander's eyes. "Tell me all, Commander. Why do you seek it? What benefit could it possibly hold?"

"Those it belongs to require its knowledge desperately. They say the Orb's knowledge holds the power that will save them from the same evil that plagues this world—knowledge that they have long lost during their absence from it."

"Say they are the Paraxidiax Goram Thosit!" begged the Curator anxiously. "Say they are the ones as in the stories told throughout the eons!"

"The same," answered the Commander. "As we speak they wait for us outside. They draw the Desolators so we may have clear passage here. But I don't know how much longer they can hold out—"

"I see them!" announced Beyruth while looking out one of the oval windows. "It is true! They are there, on the crossing bridge! They have power surpassing anything I have ever seen!"

"Show me! Show me, Commander!" begged the Curator. "Let my last sights be that of living legends."

"Help me," the Commander asked me.

Without delay the Commander and I turned the hovering septicrux and pushed it toward the window. As the Commander tilted it up, the Curator soon caught glimpse of the battle raging between the three Paraxidiax Seekers and the Desolators.

The Seekers were surely outnumbered, but it did not seem to matter. They held their ground securely. Spheres of energy were yet enveloping the Desolators and vanquishing one after another.

"The stories are true, then! The stories are true!" the Curator rejoiced.

"Yes," the Commander replied.

"Oh, and to think that I am part to blame for their possible demise, keeping their possession as a trophy of the ages," cried the Curator.

"Remember, if it were not for you, who knows where the Orb would be. It would likely still be lost to them. In a way, you've helped save them."

His friend found comfort in this perspective and smiled. "You always find the good within a situation, Commander. How I have always admired you for it." He turned to look at the Commander and uttered with a rising inner strength. "You must help them right this wrong within the universe, Commander! You will find their Orb in my vestry . . . where it has been always. Now go!"

"Good-bye, old friend," said the Commander softly.

"We can't just leave him!" I cried.

"He's dying. There's nothing we can do for him," he replied.

"You're wrong! Claire has microcellite injectors! They're right here! I have them here in her belt! They'll repair the cellular damage!"

"They won't work on him; the meld is throughout and far too severe. Maybe if we had arrived sooner, but it's too late—"

"Then a stasis inducer! We can freeze his brain in stasis until—"

"It's too late, Bishop."

"We have to try!" I pleaded.

"Trust me, Bishop. It won't work, and we've delayed long enough. We cannot be sure how much longer the Seekers can continue keeping the Desolators occupied," the Commander said firmly.

"Listen to the good Commander, child. Do not fret over me, though it is most appreciated. My shell cannot be restored no matter the technologies you possess . . . I will soon die and be released from my bondage; then my light will shine free, untouched by these Desolators . . . It is the way it is to be. Now you must leave. I insist. Go."

The Commander began to leave, as did Beyruth and I, though grudgingly. Unexpectedly, there was an additional utterance from the Curator—one that was only in earshot of me. "Child," he called.

I stopped and turned. "Yes?" I uttered apprehensively, not sure if I had heard correctly, not even sure I had actually heard anything at all.

"Something unknown to you has urged you to come on this journey," continued the Curator. "You are uncertain as to why. But know this, child. It is expected of you . . . I see great brightness within you . . . Go forth, and let the light within you shine." He smiled and struggled to continue. "Now make haste with the Commander, and may you succeed." Just then the whitening meld of the hovering septicrux reached his neck. He looked toward the window at the Seekers, and a faint smile formed on his face. The remaining life in his eyes then disappeared and his face hardened. The septicrux lowered and came to rest on the floor like a statue.

"Come on, Bishop!" called the Commander. "Let's go!"

Without further delay I hurried after the Commander, distressed by what I had just witnessed, and also somewhat bewildered as to the Curator's words of surprising truth. There had indeed been something unknown urging me to come on this journey. I wondered just how this curator knew.

THE ORB

An elevat was located in the center of a flight of wide spiral stairs. It was large, but not large enough for the Komorah.

"Take the spiral," the Commander told the Komorah. "And don't stop until you reach the top."

The Komorah acknowledged with a snort and bounded silently upward as the Commander and I entered the elevat. For his size, his speed was remarkably swift.

"Prince," called the Commander. "Remain here and keep watch on this route. If any come to ascend, come and tell us."

"Aye," acknowledged Beyruth. "Godspeed," he then wished us.

"Rise," ordered the Commander.

The Commander and I ascended in a flash. As the Komorah looked up and watched us leave, he pitched his ears back and whined. We were now far from his immediate protection.

The elevat gently came to a stop and immediately we could see all around us a large dodecagonal room from which many small curtained arches were evenly spaced. The walls were covered in a red silken tapestry. Between any two arches alternated an ornate white vase with a flamboyant black chair, followed by another vase and another chair. The ceiling was like a brilliant sky. A crystalline dome glimmered like ice, refracting beams of rainbow light on the floor and walls. It was the same crystalline dome, the same massive tower, that we had seen on our approach to the museum.

We looked over the surrounding guardrail. The Komorah was a fair distance away but advancing quickly. The Commander seemed at ease with the distance and stepped out and crept toward one of the curtained arches. His choice didn't make any particular sense to me. With the repetitive decor, the room looked the same in any position. In fact, were it not for the stairs, one could easily lose one's bearings. For anyone else, a choice would have been pure guesswork, but for the Commander, it seemed all very familiar. He slowly pulled the curtain open, looked in, and entered. I followed closely by his side.

The room was large and triangular and had the look of a scientist's laboratory. Strange apparatuses were spread out over the floor and tables and looked to be silently conducting some form of grand experiment. Three other curtained passages were located farther ahead, perhaps leading to more rooms of unknown experiments.

Before us, resting on an ornate bronze pedestal in the center of the room, was a brilliantly metallic little sphere the size of my hand.

"That it?" I asked quietly.

"It is," he replied as we slowly walked toward it.

And so this was the treasure of our hunt, the Orb, the so-called Library of All that once and still belonged to the legendary Paraxidiax Goram Thosit. It was beautiful, and it was ours.

TEMPTATION

My trip to the Paraxidiax world of solitude and the planetary isle of Dur had been acknowledged. I was now published in the *Space Exploration Journal*. I stood in the Antarctica City public square theatron and peeked out from the wing at a growing crowd. A beautiful pink sunset was smiling across at us. It was glorious.

I was waiting to receive the award of Recognition of Cosmic Discovery. I was the first to bring back proof of sentient astral life from beyond the known universe. Charlemagne Creeggan, the great professor of Tecton Field sciences, was to present the award, and I was to introduce the Paraxidiax Seekers, Komorah, and Beyruth. The Astral-Geosciences Administration was there too, wanting to know more of the worlds I visited and interview my astral friends. My greatest wishes had come true.

"Congratulations, Bishop," said a familiar voice, followed by a familiar bark. I turned. My uncle was standing there and smiling at me with Sebastian by his side. "You deserve this. You've done something extraordinary, and I'm so very proud of you."

"Thank you, Uncle," I replied. He wasn't angry at my leaving, nor was he disappointed, as I thought he might be. He was genuinely happy for me.

Sebastian wagged his tail excitedly, more than I had ever seen before. Servitude stepped forward with Morganah, holding a bouquet of wild flowers. He seemed anxious to give them to me.

"Salutations, Miss Bishop," he said.

Before I had the chance to take them, my uncle pulled me aside. He had something important to say and it was obvious it just couldn't wait.

"What is it, Uncle?" I asked.

He was on the verge of tears. "I'm sorry I was always so hard and disagreeable toward your wishes. It was just that I feared losing you . . . like your mother . . . and father."

"I know, Uncle, I know." I hugged him. "And your son, my cousin."

"Yes. Arnold."

"I'm sorry for leaving like I did."

"Don't be. It all turned out for the good. All is forgiven. You're alive and well, home and safe."

"Yes," I whispered. "Safe."

"So," he blurted, "you must introduce me to this mystery man of yours—this Commander fellow—"

"Hey, Blondie-Blue!" said another familiar voice suddenly.

"Charley!" I exclaimed. He was decked in his gleaming white LSC uniform. "What are you doing here?"

"I received orders to attend your award ceremony," he said. "That discovery of yours is the best thing that's ever happened for me."

"How? Why?" I asked bewildered.

"The LSC wants me to command the starship to explore those worlds you visited."

I looked up at him as he stood close and put his hands on my shoulders. "That's wonderful. I'm so happy for you." I hugged him tightly, having missed his presence for so long.

"But I want to ask you something," he said.

"What's that?"

He hesitated. "It was wrong of me to leave you the way I did."

"Oh, but you had your own starchasing to do, Charley."

"I know, but it wasn't right," he said sincerely.

"It happened the way it happened. No harm."

"I'd give it all up for one thing."

"Give it up? What for?" I asked ever so puzzled.

"You. I'd give it all up for you."

"Me? What do you mean?"

"Will you marry me, Bishop Alexandrah Hays?"

I was taken aback and thrilled beyond anything.

"Go on, Bishop! Say yes!" shouted Danikah, holding a pink frosted cake. Edwin stood beside her.

"Say yes, dear girl," cheered another familiar voice. I slowly turned, wondering if it were possible.

"Claire?" I questioned, "How—?"

"Shush, my dear girl," Claire replied. She stood looking at me with a pleasant smile. "All shall be revealed. Are you going to keep the young man waiting?"

"No, I—" I looked at Charley who was anxiously waiting for my answer. "Of course. Yes. I will. Yes."

I was about to kiss him when Claire took me by the arm and whispered into my ear. "I have two people who want very much to see you."

"Who?" I asked, ever so mystified.

"You'll see. Over here," she said, guiding me gently along. "Right there, dear girl, right there." Claire pointed and stepped aside.

A young man and woman approached from the darkness of the wing. The woman had long auburn hair, freckles, and green eyes, and the man had curly blond hair and blue eyes. I stared at them and studied their details, awestruck beyond belief.

"Mom? Dad?"

They smiled and held out their arms. I ran toward them and embraced them. I didn't know how, but they were alive. I closed my eyes and cried joyously, the tears streaming down my cheeks. It was all so perfect . . . Too perfect.

"But you're dead," I whispered. "Both of you are dead. How are you alive?"

They didn't answer.

"How?" I cried. "Tell me how," I begged. But they remained oddly silent. I opened my flooding eyes and saw a blurry figure ahead. As I tried to focus, the figure appeared to move closer. My parents' warmth grew colder as it came into view. It was Morganah slowly trotting toward me. On her back was the Commander, and he was glaring at me.

"Bishop," he said. "What are you doing standing there like a pillar of salt?"

I backed away. My parents began contorting their mouths attempting to speak, but only whispering breaths emerged. As I backed away farther they grew pale and stared a dead, motionless stare. They quickly withered before my eyes. I screamed and turned away in horror.

Claire stood before me, flickering as a simulated image from a messager. "You silly, hopeless girl," she said in her always-kind voice.

I turned back to the Commander. Instead, it was my uncle who approached.

"You selfish little bitch!" he yelled violently. He raised his fist and backhanded me across the face. I fell hard to the ground.

I put my hand to my throbbing cheek and looked up. Sebastian growled at me as he and my uncle approached. I crawled away, unable to find the strength to stand.

"That's right, run away! Run!" my uncle fired contemptuously. "Run away with the Commander, you little bitch!" His eyes were fierce and penetrating. He was intent on striking another blow. I found myself cornered against a wall.

"No!" I screamed. "You're not real! My real uncle Augustus would never hit me! He would never swear at me! You're not real! This is a dream!"

"That's why I ran away from you!" Charley intervened. "You're nothing but a dreamer, a starchasing little dreamer! All you're fit for is the shuttleport IT! You're a farmer! An Earthling! That's all you'll ever be!" he berated. *A cosmic explorer? An astral-terrestrial archaeologist?* he teased. "Grow up, Bishop!"

"Is that what you wished for, Bishop?" asked Danikah in a sassy tone.

"I think if she were to tell you, it wouldn't come true now, would it?" stated Edwin with a smirk.

"You could have done better, Bishop," Danikah said shaking her head.

Sebastian bit my ankle and began pulling me. Blood began to pour from the wound, and a sharp penetrating pain took over my entire body. My limbs were beginning to turn white as if they were melding with a septicrux.

"Come to safety with me, Miss Bishop!" exclaimed Servitude, holding out his hand to me. *"I will save you, Miss Bishop!"*

His head suddenly dropped off in front of me as the swipe of a scythe swung over his shoulders. My uncle shoved the body aside and was then about to swing the weapon toward me. I hid my face from the coming blade.

"Bishop!" a fractured voice echoed.

I opened my eyes.

"Bishop! Don't listen to them!" shouted the Commander. "Bishop, are you with me?!"

Very quickly I realized where I really and truly was. I was in the Curator's vestry; the Commander was ahead, and the Orb, the purpose of our being there, was before us. My uncle, Charley, Claire—my parents—all of them were an illusion— the work of a Desolator.

"I'm with you," I answered.

The Commander's hand reached and was about to take hold of the Orb when a deep mechanized voice commanded, *"Stop!"*

CONFRONTATION

A Desolator emerged from behind one of the three curtained arches.

"Identify yourselves!" it exclaimed while raising two tentacles and opening the protective shutters.

Several more Desolators emerged and began to hover around us. The Commander looked around, taking note of all of them and their every detail. Most were incomplete. The scalelike armor and most of the waving tentacles were missing, and on some, one or two of their crimson eyes was absent. Only four were present in their full glory. They were without a doubt the original Desolators that had arrived on this world.

"Identify yourselves!" the Desolator again demanded.

The Commander suddenly grinned and calmly turned while keeping his hand over the Orb. "Bishop Alexandrah Hays," he introduced. "I'm the Commander," he declared sharply.

A moment of uncertainty followed, as though they were having difficulty processing the answer.

"Commander?" another complete Desolator questioned in surprise. *"You are the Commander?"*

"In person!" he declared. "Didn't expect me, did you?"

"Impossible! You are dead!" the first exclaimed.

"Am I?" retorted the Commander.

"You were to have been caught in the holds of Abussos."

"Was I? Good. You're hallucinating, then. Pretend I'm not here!"

"Silence!" ordered the Desolator. *"You will prove yourself!"*

"Prove myself?" he queried.

"If you declare to be the Commander, then you will prove yourself!"

The Commander glanced around. "You're worse off than I thought," he uttered in surprise. "All right, then." He smiled and then contorted his expression to an intense raging anger. "Search your chaotic minds and look at my face, Desolators! Recollect! Helena, Curlan Drift, Dianavis, Braepoint Strand, Shurengga!" He turned and stared into each of the Desolators' glaring crimson eyes, and with each name his voice became louder. "Abagemnon, Hurtic, Balasalesh! Shall I continue?"

"He is the Commander!" one of the incomplete Desolators exclaimed. *"He is the Commander of the tenth legion! The Commander of Megeddon! He is the bringer of doom!"*

"Yes!" sneered the Commander.

All but the first of the Desolators suddenly moved back. *"He is nothing!"* it declared. *"He shall be eradicated!"* As the able Desolators aimed their tentacles toward the Commander, he quickly grabbed the Orb from the pedestal.

"Kill me and you'll destroy the Orb!" the Commander shouted as he held it up.

The Desolators immediately directed their weapons toward me.

"Kill her, touch her, and *I'll* destroy the Orb!" he shouted while holding his disruptor against it. "Either way, the Orb will

152

be no more! And it *is* what you've been attempting to unlock the secrets of, isn't it?"

The Desolators didn't answer.

"Isn't it?" demanded the Commander.

"*Yes,*" one of the Desolators replied.

"*Silence!*" the first Desolator exclaimed.

The Commander grinned. "Now answer me this!" he demanded. "How did you escape from Abussos? Its gravity swallowed everything!"

"*Silence!*" the Desolator exclaimed again, but this time the words were directed toward the Commander in a seething rage. "*We are Desolators! We do not answer to the likes of you!*"

"How?!" raged the Commander.

A long moment of silence filled the room. Then, against the Desolator's own instruction, it answered.

"*Unknown. We awoke from our sleep to find ourselves . . . adrift.*"

"And you're lost!" the Commander mocked.

One of the incomplete Desolators edged its tentacles toward me. I quickly grabbed the antigravity emitter from the Commander's belt and pointed it toward the threat. The Desolator's tentacles quickly retreated.

"You okay there?" asked the Commander unflinchingly.

"Yeah, fine," I nervously replied.

"Good girl," he swiftly praised.

The Desolators remained silent, some swaying their tentacles from me to the Commander, and back again.

"You don't know what to do, do you?" the Commander smirked.

"*Silence!*" the first Desolator exclaimed deeply.

"You're lost, and without orders!"

"*Our orders are as always. To ERADICATE!*" it screamed.

The Commander laughed. "*Really?* There was a time when you would never have left any of the creatures on this world alive, and yet they are! There was a time when you would never leave a building standing or a tree growing, yet they're untouched!" He paused and looked at the surrounding Desolators. "You saw life and began harvesting it the first moment you got here, attempting to rebuild your numbers and find your way to the next inhabited world! Trouble is, there were too many fresh minds to mold from too many far away worlds, with no Tribune within your ranks to put order to them! Now you lack the intelligence and experience of your original collective! You're incomplete!"

"*Silence!*" commanded the Desolator.

"*Yessss,* the truth hurts, doesn't it? You've become confused, inefficient, compromised!" continued the Commander fearlessly. "Look at you." He stared at the most incomplete Desolator. "Forced to serve when your birth is incomplete! But there's an inkling of hope, isn't there? A small glimmer! You discovered this here, *the Orb,*" he said tauntingly. "You think it will hold the answers to your questions and give you direction!"

Another complete and original Desolator, replied reluctantly, "*Yes.*"

"*Silence!*" commanded the first Desolator.

"Now I've got it," teased the Commander. "And *what* are you going to do?"

"*You will be eradicated!*" one of the incomplete Desolators said.

"*No!*" replied the first. "*The Orb is paramount! It must not be harmed!*"

The Desolators moved toward us.

"Komorah, come!" shouted the Commander.

The Desolators halted their approach and turned in several directions to investigate the Commander's summons. The moments that passed seemed like an eternity as we all waited for the Komorah to show himself, but strangely, he wasn't coming.

Was he confused as to which room to enter? Was he still climbing the twist of stairs? Or had he suddenly abandoned us? Or, God forbid, was he dead?

With concern building, I looked at the Commander. The Commander looked around at the surrounding Desolators. He too was becoming noticeably concerned.

The Desolators resumed their approach.

RUN!

Spontaneously, I activated the antigravity emitter and sent one of the approaching Desolators somersaulting across the room, crashing through one of the walls. The others slowly backed away.

The Desolator righted itself and stepped through the hole in the wall. As I anticipated my demise, an overwhelming confidence filled my heart—a profound fearlessness emerged and a defiant righteousness. Perhaps that was what the Curator had meant when he told me to let the light that he saw within me shine. Maybe it was none other than my inner courage.

"Stay back!" I shouted defiantly.

As the Desolator stepped closer, it raised several of its tentacles, opened the protective shutters, and began fixing aim toward me.

"*They must not be harmed whilst the Commander possesses the Orb!*" the first Desolator announced.

"*She will be eradicated!*" the approaching Desolator thundered angrily.

"*She—will—not!*" the other argued.

"Komorah!" shouted the Commander at the top of his lungs.

The approaching Desolator ignored its comrade and suddenly dispersed a ray toward me. The glimmer was instantaneous, but there was ample time to notice that the beam arced away and through the wall. The Desolator dispersed another ray, but again the beam arced away. The heat from the rays was intense, and two perfect holes were left smoldering in the wall. Something unknown was pulling the dispersion of energy away from its intended target. I stared in awe at the unexpected result. The Commander grinned, knowing full well it was the proper outcome.

Suddenly the wall exploded inward with the Komorah violently pushing his way through. As he stomped in, he took an immediate swipe toward two of the Desolators. His mace smashed through the first and deeply crushed the armor of the other. As they were flung across the room, releasing a bloody splatter, he bellowed a victorious cry.

He looked winded from his climb up the endless spiral of stairs, but there was plenty more fight within him. As the other Desolators began dispersing their rays toward him, the beams were inexplicably absorbed into the head of the mace, as if it were some magnet or vacuum that hungered for the intense energy that was being emitted.

The Komorah roared in intense anger and seemed to utter partially intelligible words to the Commander and me, instructing us to "Leave. Go. Be quick."

"Run!" the Commander yelled.

The Komorah began battling the Desolators as we dashed through the hole in the wall. I turned and watched the Komorah being grabbed and overpowered by a mass of angry tentacles that were attempting to remove the mace from his grasp.

I activated the emitter and sent two of the Desolators spiralling away, inadvertently causing the Komorah to suffer several deep scrapes from the array of departing tentacles. Once free, the Komorah struck a finishing blow to a third attacking Desolator—the mace absorbing the beams from the others that were approaching.

As we ran toward the stairs, Beyruth darted up. "They're coming! They're coming!" he announced fearfully, then, discovering the perilous situation at hand. "Oh, slek! We're done for!"

"No, we're not!" returned the Commander. He looked at the Komorah, who was relentlessly swinging his mace and smashing any who dared come near.

All that was left now were the incomplete ones, unable to defend or attack. To me, they still posed an imminent threat. I activated the emitter once more and waved it across the room, sending the defenseless Desolators through the walls one by one. The Commander watched with a rejoicing glimmer in his eyes, but there was little time to cheer. It was time to turn our backs and our attention toward our only way out.

"Bishop! That's enough!" he bellowed. "We're done here! Let's go!"

Barely half a step had been taken by any of us when a Desolator burst from beneath the elevat and pushed away the fragments. In its full glory it hovered and readied its tentacles toward the Commander.

"*Ah!*" the Commander blurted as he held the disruptor to the Orb.

"*You will relinquish the Orb!*" the Desolator declared.

There was a momentary pause.

"Bishop," the Commander quickly uttered.

His simple utterance—the tone in which he said my name—told me what I must do. I moved my thumb, activated the emitter, and instantaneously pushed the Desolator through several walls and outside. Daylight poured in through the gaping hole.

"Good girl!" exclaimed the Commander as he looked down the stairs to see several more Desolators on their way up. Some were walking; others were rising up the central shaft.

As we jogged down the stairs, I held the emitter ready and gave an occasional burst toward any Desolator who pushed too close for comfort. Those that I missed were swiftly dealt with by the Komorah's deadly swipes, leaving the mutilated hulls to tumble lifelessly to the bottom of the stairs. With the movement of the Komorah's swinging mace, the offensive beams that were attracted to it mysteriously arced around us as if consciously trying to avoid contact.

While some Desolators wanted to eradicate us, others remained noticeably hesitant; an incessant quarrelling transpired between them. Mixed phrases of *We must not destroy the Orb* versus *They must, shall, will be eradicated* repeated endlessly, becoming a deafening and confused babble.

When we reached the bottom, where the piled lifeless shells and tangle of tentacles lay in a spreading pool of translucent red Desolator blood, there was no end in sight to the Desolators that were closing in from all directions. The Commander directed the way into a wide corridor and toward the main doors of the museum. I looked behind and saw the long reach of a Desolator's tentacle snagging the Komorah's ankle, sending him to the floor. I aimed the emitter and thrust the Desolator through the wall. In that brief moment, the advance of Desolators ahead of us had been momentarily forgotten.

"Bishop!" yelled the Commander. "Now would be a most excellent time!"

I turned to look and inadvertently ran into a large display cabinet protruding from the wall. I spun toward the floor, sending the emitter flying from my hand. The Komorah pinched my tunic, gently and easily picking me up and setting me on my feet without breaking his momentum.

We watched in despair as the emitter glided toward the fast-approaching Desolators. If they got hold of it, they would surely destroy it, and if they destroyed it, it would surely bring an end to our escape. Another threat by the Commander to destroy the Orb himself would likely not hold the Desolators back—too many were possessed with the urge to kill, even if it meant their own ruin.

However small and unlikely, it was Beyruth who saved us. Like an arrow, he shot toward the emitter and tightly grabbed hold of it. The Desolators now directed their rays at him and continued without success—the beams bent up and over and then wound around the Commander and me, finally hitting the Komorah's mace. With all the strength Beyruth could muster, he lifted the emitter and returned it to me. He then stared at the Desolators and grinned victoriously at his momentous deed.

In those few seconds of uncertainty, it was the solidarity displayed between newly acquainted friends from across the cosmos that reigned supreme. When one faltered, another was there to protect them—all sharing one heart and one mind and striving toward one goal: to survive!

ERADICATED

Several Desolators somersaulted through the museum's main doors as I launched them away with the emitter. A second later, the Commander and I ran out, our giant protector bounding quickly behind. Beyruth followed alongside, evading the Komorah's swing toward a Desolator.

The crackling sound of electrical surges could be heard over the bridge, where the trio of Paraxidiax Seekers was still battling the Desolators. Multiple Desolators continued disappearing within the forming and then shrinking spheres of energy, and with each forming sphere, the grass and leaves of the closest trees withered into crisp remnants of what had once been thriving life.

A blast of something unknown stung our eyes and noses as we approached the bridge. The air became increasingly difficult to breathe, and the grass turned to dust under our feet.

"It burns!" cried Beyruth. "I cannot see! I cannot . . . breathe!"

"Take hold of my collar!" I struggled as I placed Claire's respirator over my face.

"It's ozonic ionization!" explained the Commander, who himself was suffering the effects. "They're depleting the ambient energy!"

It was a lengthy jog toward the bridge, but as we neared, I no longer needed to make constant use of the emitter, nor the Komorah his mace. We were now under the close protection of the Seekers.

"Commander! We must return to your vessel!" said Onu in a quick series of loud clicks and murmurs. "To unleash the full extent of our power may destroy it! The energy knows no boundaries!"

Then, a realization set in. "It's going to be a long hike back with a pack of demented Desolators following us, isn't it, Commander?" I puffed tiredly.

But the Commander did not appear to be listening. He seemed preoccupied, as though he were waiting for something to happen around us.

"Do not fear, Bishop Alexandrah Hays," assured Sodu. "All will remain within the protection of our barrier whilst we retreat! We will relinquish it and restore it around you! Come!"

"Wait!" shouted the Commander as the thundering crack of a sonic explosion followed. He smiled as he looked up and pointed toward the sky. "The Dee-Dee comes to us!"

I watched as the Dee-Dee hovered above, casting its shadow over us like an eclipse. It had been what the Commander was waiting for, the reason for his preoccupied state of mind. He knew from experience that the Dee-Dee would come. He knew she would not leave us to arduously venture back on our own, thus risking all our gains for nothing.

Thank God for a conscious ship, I thought as the Dee-Dee's ramp opened like the mouth of some great, glimmering whale.

Suddenly my thoughts of a living ship didn't seem so peculiar after all. It was, for sure, a welcome sight.

"Do what you intend here, Paraxidiax!" barked the Commander. *"Eradicate them!"*

"We must first encompass your vessel, Commander," clicked and murmured Sodu.

"Komorah, guard!" instructed Onu, while pulling the staff from the wall of the energy barrier. It sparkled and disappeared as the Komorah bellowed a warrior cry toward the Desolators, daring any to come forth. From the relentless rays being absorbed, the head of the Komorah's mace began to glow a vibrant blue.

The trees began to crack and splinter, and limbs began to fall. Every last iota of ambient energy was being exhumed by the Seekers. Struggling vigorously to reestablish the barrier around us and the Dee-Dee, the Seekers were very quickly becoming exhausted. The newly forming barrier seemed far too large to stabilize despite their efforts. It flickered erratically as some of the rays from the Desolators struck it, while others passed through and were drawn into the Komorah's mace.

"It's not going to hold!" shouted the Commander.

A Desolator dared to move forward, seemingly to take advantage of the disengaged barrier and challenge the Komorah. It was then instantly severed in half as the barrier flickered back into existence, leaving the mutilated astral head within its armored shell to spill out from a membrane of translucent blood. Just as quickly as it had appeared in that opportune moment, the barrier again faded away.

Suddenly the Komorah bellowed an agonizing cry and dropped his mace. His hand was smoldering. The energy the mace had consumed had produced an intense heat beyond the giant's tolerance. In the split second that followed, one of the Seekers was touched by a ray. The white light momentarily enveloped its body and then transformed it into a pale gray dust that drifted away in the air like a ghostly image. Remnants of the Seeker's burnished cloak, along with the partially disintegrated defensive shields, fell to the ground.

Instantly the two remaining Seekers resumed their defense and enclosed us all within a smaller barrier. As the mace lay there, its bluish glow rapidly diminished, no longer attracting the beams that were still being dispersed. It was difficult at first to ascertain which of the Seekers had met its demise. All anyone really knew was that one of them was no more. The Komorah was the first to perhaps realize which of his three masters had been eradicated. While holding the wrist of his burnt hand, he looked to where his master had been standing and gave a foreboding whine. It was Sertu.

The Desolators were now directing their rays at the barrier in a continuous, almost synchronized manner.

"Annihilation is impossible! We have not the strength to hold an adequate barrier without our complete complement!" declared Sodu in a speedy series of clicks and murmurs. "We grow weak."

"Yes," added Onu. "I . . . am about to fail."

"Komorah, guard!" instructed Sodu.

Without apprehension, the Komorah picked up his still searing mace as Onu fell to the ground. The barrier faded, leaving the giant to once more take responsibility for the safety of all by again absorbing the rays into his mace.

I resumed use of the emitter, pushing away advancing Desolators while retreating onto the Dee-Dee's ramp along with Sodu.

"Bishop!" called the Commander, drawing my attention as he threw me the Orb. He then slung Onu over his shoulder and picked up the staff.

With arms outstretched, Sodu created a large sphere of energy around several of the nearest Desolators. With a flick of the wrists, the sphere, along with the Desolators, shrank into nothingness. A blast of ozone hit everyone. It was then, in this last act, when Sodu collapsed and came to hang limply over the edge of the ramp; completely exhausted from the enigmatic ability to harness the equally enigmatic energy.

Beyruth, who was still clinging to me, began gasping intensely.

"Komorah, come!" shouted the Commander.

There were now only a few Desolators left, perhaps twenty-five or thirty at most, compared to the hundreds before. Most were incomplete, but all were still a viable threat and more than enough to bring a quick end to our departure, were it not for the Komorah. The Commander waited for the Komorah before stepping onto the ramp. The Desolators closed in. One by one, I pushed them back.

"*We must recover the Orb!*" a Desolator thundered. "*Synchronize dispersion! Focus on the vessel!*"

"*Focus on the female!*" argued another. "*She possesses the Orb!*"

"*The Orb must not be destroyed!*" another argued. "*Focus on the vessel! It is their only means of escape!*"

As the Commander entered alpha hold beside me, the ramp began to close. The Komorah bounded toward us, dragged his limp master up the ramp, and began to whine. One of his hands was badly burnt, and the other was smoldering.

A Desolator came forward and attempted to hold the ramp open. A second came forth to assist; both were reaching and waving their tentacles, trying desperately to get in and grab at anything. A third appeared and reached for the Commander. It snapped a grazing nip against the back of his leg and immediately recoiled for another strike. The Commander turned and thrust Onu's staff into the mouth of the claw. A white spark flashed, causing the Desolator to retract.

Simultaneously, the Komorah thrust his glowing mace forward and into the glaring eye of one of the Desolators, pushing it back as I activated the emitter and forced the other away. The ramp sealed shut.

The Komorah dropped his mace and roared in excruciating pain while clenching his wrist. He snorted heavily as pieces of burnt flesh dangled from his hand and dropped to the floor.

Grinding and hammering thuds against the Dee-Dee's hull began. I was the only one to really take any notice as the Commander tossed the staff onto the floor and carefully laid Onu beside it. No one else seemed concerned. Understandably, the Komorah was too consumed with pain, the two Paraxidiax Seekers were comatose, and Beyruth . . . Where was Beyruth? I could no longer feel him clinging onto my tunic for dear life, nor hear his wheezing behind my ear.

I turned and found him on the floor. I ripped the respirator from my face and threw it aside. "Commander!" I uttered frantically.

"Don't worry, she'll hold," assured the Commander, assuming that my concern was directed at the hammering thuds of the Desolators.

"No! It's Beyruth!" I cried. "I think he's dead!"

"Take him to the dispensary!" he instructed.

To know which way one is going,
one must learn,
for without learning,
one is forever lost.

Ackard the Wise Man
AM 7070

REFLECTIONS OVER A
TURBULENT CEE

While Beyruth lay encased in the revitalization chamber, I leaned back against the wall across from him and watched dolefully for any change. Deep in thought, I mulled over our adventure and began to cry. It had been too much: the drowned Perinthian, the severed heads, the Curator, the Seeker, the nightmare temptation that had almost overtaken me, and now Beyruth, who hovered close to death. All the sights and sounds flashed through my mind over and over. *What am I doing here?* I kept asking.

Though there had been that unknown drive for me to explore other worlds, in reflection, I had only myself to blame. The Commander had warned me about the potential dangers, but no, I had been determined to partake; I had truly wanted nothing else. I now had to deal with it. But how? How could I? How could I put it all into perspective? It was all too indescribable, far too overwhelming.

The only thing in my life that had ever been remotely similar was when an occasional lamb was found half devoured by a pack of hungry roving wolves. That was all part of what the life of a farmer was. I had grown up with that. No matter how awful such a sight was, I was used to that. It was imperfectly perfect. How could I put order to all this? How could I make sense of it? My mind was racing.

"Think happy thoughts," I said to myself. I had to think of my friends, think of Charley, think of the farm—my home. Yes. And there was Sebastian and Morganah, Servitude, and my uncle Augustus—and there was his attitude toward my starchasing aspirations. I should have listened to him. Right now I could be at home. I could be working the fields, repairing the drones, safe . . . my life, uneventful. He was no doubt missing me, no doubt wondering where on Earth—rather, where in the *universe*—I was. What if I had been killed like the lamb in the field? Or *eradicated*, like Sertu? I'd never see my uncle again. *He* would never see *me* again. That thought bothered me more. My happy thoughts weren't helping. They were transforming into unhappy thoughts. They were bordering on despair. They were, like Desolators, attempting to overwhelm me. I felt so weak.

"Patient is stabilizing," a melodic voice from the revitalization chamber suddenly confirmed.

I continued to cry, though now joyously, as I wiped the tears from my cheeks. To hear such words was a tremendous relief. Beyruth wasn't to be added to the memorial of those lost in today's misadventure. *This* was the bit I needed to bring me back on track. *It's not all bad*, I thought. *In retrospect, it could have been worse—much worse.* My thoughts again were dwelling upon the negatives of what was and what might have been. I stopped myself. No! I would have none of that. "Buck up, Bishop," I whispered to myself. *You just helped save a Perinthian Prince. You helped a race of long-departed astral-terrestrials seeking to recover their long-lost library, and in that, you've helped save them. Now*

*get out there and see what more you can do. Let the light the Curator
saw within you shine, Bishop Hays!*

I stepped out of the dispensary and marched toward alpha
hold. The Komorah had his eyes closed and was breathing
heavily due to his wounds. I removed a microcellite injector
from the pouch on my belt and was about to place the tiny
metallic disc on his arm. He shifted away, surprised by my
sudden closeness. He hadn't heard me come in.

"It's all right," I said softly. "It's a microcellite injector. The
microcellites are cellular drones. They'll help heal the wounds
faster."

The giant watched me place and then gently press the
metallic disc onto the back of his wrist. A blue light on it
changed to yellow.

"They travel through your body and repair what's wrong.
When they're done, they'll travel back and into the injector."

He then looked at the burns on his hands. Before his eyes,
ever so slowly, the burns began to heal, the cuts on his arms
began to seal over, and even the oozing callus on his leg began
to mend.

"The light will change to green when they're done. They
won't do much for the scars, I'm afraid. Unfortunately, that's
another type of medicine I don't have."

The Komorah replied gruffly and unexpectedly. "Like scars.
Respect scars. Remind me of battles won . . . and companions
lost."

I forcefully smiled as the Komorah turned to watch over his
Masters. "How are they?" I asked.

"Weak," answered the Komorah. "Rejuvenation is slow."

"If there is anything that can be done, let me know," I said.
All I could really do was offer a caring intent. After all, they
were astrals. How could *I* help them "rejuvenate"? What did *I*

know about their astral physiology? What could *I* do that the Komorah could not? It was a meaningless offer, really, only uttered in kindness. I felt sorry for him. It was obvious that the great giant was feeling a certain responsibility for the fate of one of his Masters. If he hadn't dropped the mace, Sertu would still be alive.

I casually held a knuckle to my nose and turned around. I wanted to stay longer but his smell was getting to me. I then spotted my respirator by my feet and picked it up. To wear it in his presence and stay, I thought, would be rude. I was about to leave but further curiosity made me stop.

"You speak my language," I said, "without the help of the Commander's ship."

"Indeed . . . I speak many . . . tongues. One is that of the . . . first world. It has been ... a long time. And it has changed some."

"Everyone keeps saying that—first world. Why?"

"It is because . . . it is."

I was intent on asking the Commander to shed more light on the matter. As I reached the bridge, I heard his voice. I couldn't quite make out what he was saying, but his tone had a certain air of seriousness about it. When I entered, I found him standing in front of the forward console, staring out the panoramic window. I could now hear him plainly.

"Until further notice Dur-Cee has been placed under the Keyhurquiem alert status—section one, subsection three, paragraph nine. All inhabitants and visitors who did not escape are presumed dead. Do not under any circumstances investigate." He touched some shaded shapes on the console.

"What are you doing?" I asked.

"Leaving a universal alert beacon . . . so no one'll visit."

A familiar swift swishing sound occurred. An elongated pod shot from view and faded quickly into the depths of space. The Commander continued to watch the console.

"How's the Prince?" he asked.

"He's going to be okay."

"Good." He glanced at me quickly and noticed my reddish eyes. He could tell I had been crying. "How are *you* doing?"

"Fine." I paused. "Good," I reaffirmed.

"Good girl."

There was a long period of silence as the Commander remained on vigilant watch over the console.

"Commander," I calmly and inquisitively uttered.

"Mm," he returned.

"What will happen to the Desolators we left on the planet?"

"Well, they have no Tribune, and they're enraged with internal conflict—thanks to a little additional help from myself." He grinned briefly. "If they don't begin turning on each other first, they'll soon fall dormant."

With one curiosity having replaced another, I almost forgot what I had intended to ask. "Tell me about the first world. The Komorah said—"

Suddenly the Dee-Dee began to shake.

"What's that?" I bellowed with worry, immediately believing that the Commander's ill-intended words toward the Desolators had somehow summoned their return. An intense swirl of white light reached out in front of us and cast a blinding glare throughout the bridge.

The Commander squinted. "Solar flare," he answered, slamming the shaded square to close the window and stepping away toward the central console. "Nothing serious. I'm regenerating the Dee-Dee's power supply again. She's hungry." The glowing golden sphere that was the Displacement Drive was, at this time, concealed by the cylinders for regeneration. He touched some shaded circles on the console. An image of Cee appeared over the central console.

"Along with the great distances we've traveled these past few days, those Desolators drained a good deal of energy from her. We should be good to go in a few minutes. The energy's nice and ripe here."

The Dee-Dee shook as another flare erupted.

"But finding the right orbital distance is posing a challenge," he said, diligently studying the floating image. "There's a lot of erratic solar turbulence to compensate for, which is odd . . . Cee's normally a well-mannered ball of flatulence . . ." He expanded the image, focusing closer within the sun. "There's an unusual irregularity in the polarity that's never been here before."

I looked at the image. "There seems to be three distinct poles," I noted with bewilderment.

"Looks like Cee's centrosphere has been shifted," said the Commander, puzzled.

"Something to do with those Tectonic rifts, maybe?"

"Possible. I had noticed a mild shift in Phoebus. It kept fuzzing up the Dee-Dee's cosmic bearings. I had to keep recalibrating, like now. This is much worse, though." He passed his hand through the image. "Rifts in the Tecton field could be the cause all right. Good observation, my dear Bishop," he complimented.

"Is it serious?"

"Things should realign and return to normal."

MY DECISION

The two Seekers were still lying motionless in alpha hold as the Dee-Dee's ramp opened to the great courtyard of the ancient Paraxidiax library.

"They're still resting," I said.

I stood beside the Komorah and removed the microcellite injector from his wrist. The microcellites had done their job. The light was green, and the Komorah's injuries were fully healed, save for a few scars.

"You can keep it," I said. "You might need it again. I have others."

The Commander knelt beside Onu. "Awake, Master Seeker," he said, gently touching Onu on the shoulder.

Onu stirred and slowly sat up as the Commander walked over to Sodu and repeated the process.

"Awake, Seeker," he said. "Let us not keep your brethren waiting."

With the aid of the Komorah, the Seekers soon stood and took a moment to compose themselves. Onu immediately took note of the library outside.

"We thank you for your assistance, Commander, and you, Bishop Alexandrah Hays," said Onu, while taking hold of the staff and Orb offered by the Komorah. "It is imperative now that we depart company and begin our passage home."

"What about sending your people the information they need?" I asked.

"As our third is no more, we cannot summon the knowledge from the Orb. We must have three to undertake this process."

"Can't one of us help?" I asked.

"The Orb was designed only for use by our kind. It has never before been attempted with a mind of an outsider. It is unknown what harm the connection may have on you."

"Well, if the Dee-Dee is faster than your ship, we can return you home," I said eagerly.

The Seekers remained silent, as if they were uncertain of the offer, but the reason for their silence was soon revealed to be none other than obvious embarrassment.

"We do not know where home is," murmured Onu. "Our memory of these coordinates was erased, and by design, our vessel is unable to reveal its record of travel."

"Yes," Sodu agreed. "Even if one were to follow our vessel's return home, it would surely destroy them."

"Yes," agreed Onu. "This was to prevent those that we might encounter on our journey from discovering our origin, and thus meeting our current fate with these Desolators." Every precaution was taken to ensure our separation."

Sodu's head lowered. "Perhaps too much so."

"I volunteer," the Commander said eagerly. "I will be your third."

"It is a possibility that you will not survive the connection," Onu replied. "The transference would then fail, and you would be calmed. We are most grateful for your willingness to assist in our plight, but we cannot allow this fate to fall unto you."

"I insist. If you leave the Desolators to plague your world longer than necessary, there may be no recovery from their devastation," declared the Commander. "I beg of you, for the sake of your existence *and* of others' across this universe, let me take the risk and help you bring an end to their threat."

Onu looked at Sodu. They looked at one another without even the slightest change of expression. It was as if they were communicating by way of telepathy. Onu looked back at the Commander. "You speak with much truth and reason, Commander. We will accept your offer only if your companion grants consent. Without it, we will not proceed," Onu asserted firmly.

"If anything were to happen to me, I know Bishop Hays would not hold blame against you," expressed the Commander with certainty.

"Bishop Hays's words, Commander. Bishop Hays must speak."

"She is your companion. She must have equal say," stated Sodu. "It is our way."

All eyes were suddenly on me. I had to be the one to decide the fate of the Commander, the possible fate of these astrals and their world—and seemingly the entire universe, for that matter. To actually have the final decision somehow thrust upon me in this way was unexpected and burdensome. I didn't want to risk losing the Commander, but at the same time I didn't want the responsibility of these Desolators destroying a civilization and expanding toward others, either. What if they reached Earth and the colonies? That would be unacceptable.

I had seen their ways, and they were certainly in no way favorable. I knew exactly what I was about to say. The choice was an easy one, but it was saying it for all to hear that was the difficult part.

"Sh-sure," I uttered insecurely. "Yes," I then asserted.

The Commander gave a slight grin toward me, his eyes sparkling with self-righteous confidence.

"So it has been said, so it shall be done," said Onu.

THE COMMANDER'S FINAL DEED

The Seekers led the way through the darkened halls of the library and into its even darker depths. We finally emerged from between a pair of columns and into a chamber with multiple arches. The columns and arches were softly illuminated by starlight cast downward through an opening in the vaulted ceiling high above. So too were three open sarcophagi that stood upright and were equally spaced around the chamber, each under an arch.

"These were resting places of the Grandmasters," clicked and murmured Onu.

Unmistakably we were standing in the heart of the grand library. In the center of this chamber, a tall, narrow pedestal and an arrangement of three curved rods extended from the floor. Each of the rods was split in two and was attached to short rails, all of which partially encompassed the pedestal. Positioned in front of each was a smoothly hewn block of stone.

Onu passed the staff to the Komorah, stepped between two of the rails, and then, carefully, placed the Orb onto the pedestal. The pedestal was undoubtedly the home of the Orb before uncertain events had taken it away. It was now home at long last, resting regally like a primary jewel in an emperor's crown.

"Who would think it would be something that could contain so much knowledge, so much importance," I whispered to the Commander. "It seems so insignificant."

"I know," he replied.

"Do as we do, Commander," Onu instructed.

The clicks and murmurs of the Master Seeker's speech echoed endlessly within the arches.

"Step forward upon the mount. Take hold as we do."

Onu and Sodu each stepped onto a separate stone block and took hold of the rail in front. The Commander did the same, and the three of them were then all evenly spaced around and facing the Orb, as if they were going to worship it in some obscure manner. Onu and Sodu closed their eyes.

"Allay your mind," continued Onu. "Ponder not upon dark things, nor ponder upon good. Focus only upon the Orb. Only then will you achieve connection with the Orb."

The Commander closed his eyes and remained still. "How will I know?" he asked.

"You will know," murmured Onu.

"You will feel," clicked Sodu.

A few seconds passed, and the Commander lowered his head ever so slightly, as if he were just beginning to fall asleep. Suddenly he lifted his head and quietly gasped. It was no doubt the result of the connection.

Onu continued. "Focus upon the question . . . upon the nature of the problem . . . upon the manner in which to solve the dilemma . . . and embrace it . . . for it is the way . . . to enable . . . transference."

A lengthy silence followed as the Komorah and I watched with great intrigue, and then the Orb began to glow. A fine static charge momentarily flashed between it and each of the Seekers' heads. I jolted in response, startled by the unexpected occurrence. Another charge flashed, this time at the Commander's head. Suddenly the Commander arched his back and tensed as if he were being electrocuted.

"Comman—" I began to call then silenced myself, thinking it best not to disturb the esoteric process. To do so might render the process void or cause harm to one of them, I thought.

The Commander's eyes opened. Vibrant beams of light shot out from them. The Orb's glow increased and filled the chamber, the brightness displaying the intricate designs on the vast arches and columns that supported the vaulted structure.

The brightness yet increased. Soon the chamber was aglow with white energy. The Seekers and the Commander were now only faint gray silhouettes and still fading ever so quickly. The intensity of the light far surpassed even the flares of Cee.

The Komorah cried out as we shielded our eyes from the blinding light. A piercing ring then sounded for a moment and silenced. The light then quickly faded as though it was being pulled back into the Orb, reclaimed as if it were some life energy too precious to waste.

The light gleaming from the Commander's eyes slowly dimmed. Onu and Sodu stood still and lowered their hands from the rail. The Commander then collapsed.

"Commander!" I cried out as I ran toward him. "Commander, are you all right?"

He wasn't moving, and his open eyes were bloodred. The transference process seemed to have caused a massive optic hemorrhage. I checked for a pulse. There was no heartbeat, and he didn't appear to be breathing.

"Commander!" I cried. "Commander, can you hear me?" I began rocking him, hoping that he would come to life. "You're not dead, are you, Commander? Tell me you're not dead!" I pleaded.

He remained still, unaffected by my determined attempts to wake him. I quickly took a microcellite injector from my pouch and placed it on his neck. The light changed from the ready blue to operating yellow . . . and then to red, indicating the patient was deceased.

"No, no, come on!" I pressed the injector again. The process repeated. The red light returned.

The microcellite had one additional setting: electric shock. I pressed the button and pulled my hand away. The Commander's body momentarily tensed. I instantly pinched his nose, opened his mouth and kissed a breath of life into him. The light on the injector changed from operating yellow to red. He still wasn't breathing and there was still no heartbeat. I pressed it again.

Shock . . . another kiss . . . operating yellow . . . red light. Over and over I continued, but my efforts were in vain.

"He is . . . I believe . . . dead," said the Komorah.

"A stasis inducer!" I bellowed. I took one of the white rectangular devices from my belt pouch and put it on the nape of the Commander's neck. "It will place his brain in stasis until we can return to the Dee-Dee and place him in a revitalization chamber!"

Like the microcellite injector, the stasis inducer light went from blue to yellow to red. Thinking I might have been doing it wrong, I adjusted the inducer over his neck and waited.

Blue . . . yellow . . . "Stay, stay, stay, please, God, make it stay," I uttered. Red. It meant that there was nothing viable to place in stasis and nothing viable for the revitalization chamber to repair. "Help me! It's not working!" I bellowed. "Commander! Don't do this to me! Please!" I begged as I clenched his tunic into my hands. "Please, Commander!" I laid my head down and cried into his chest.

The Komorah placed his hand on my shoulder. The two Seekers stepped forward.

"I fear the Commander has been . . . irreparably calmed, Bishop Hays," said Onu.

"No!" I wept. "Please, God, no."

"The Commander will be honored among the Paraxidiax Goram Thosit," Onu stated with certainty.

"Yes," agreed Sodu, "his deed shall be honored with great reverence."

"No!" I cried.

How could it be that the Commander could succumb to such an untimely end as this? He had survived over four thousand cycles and countless adventures that were surely beyond the dangers of this act of devotion. Even though the Paraxidiax Master had given warning, I couldn't believe that the danger had held true. Across the great plains of the cosmos, we had survived a horde of demented Desolators, a feat that had held moments of certain death. Why hadn't the Commander perished then in the heat of battle? Why now in this serene, peaceful setting? The Commander had perished before I really and truly got to know him, and it was all my fault. Why had I said yes when I could have said no? Damn the greater good!

GOOD-BYE

A scant whisper carried through the chamber. I looked at the
Commander.

"Commander?" I queried uncertainly.

He remained motionless. I looked around and up toward
the vaulted ceiling and the skyward opening. What I had heard
must have been simply a figment of my imagination.

"I heard it too," clicked and murmured Onu softly.

"As did I," murmured Sodu.

Again, I looked down at the Commander. His eyes were
healed and now were without any sign of injury. He had a slight
smile on his face.

"Unbelievable," the Commander whispered.

I was awestruck. I was certain my mind was playing a
terrible yet wonderful trick on me. I seriously wondered if the
Desolators' whispers were having some kind of residual effect
or if maybe, right now, I was under the spell of their whispers.
Maybe this was all an illusion.

"All the knowledge being passed through one's
consciousness—to absorb it all is virtually impossible," the

Commander quietly prattled on in amused amazement, like all was otherwise normal.

"Are you all right, Commander?" I begged.

He looked at me as if it were a ridiculous question. "Never better." He smiled and blinked. "Eyes are a little itchy."

"This isn't a Desolator's trick?"

"Certainly not!" exclaimed the Commander. He then pinched me on the arm.

"Ow!" I exclaimed.

"Would a Desolator do that?"

"I thought you were dead!" I lamented as I pounded him on the chest.

The Commander grunted. "Dead? Dead? Hey now, come on—have a little faith. You didn't think I'd pack in my kit that easily, did you?" he teased as he picked himself up and left me kneeling on the floor in awe. "There's things to be done, places to be going." He pulled the microcellite injector and stasis inducer from his neck. "These must be yours," he said and handed them to me. He then smacked his lips together. "Did you kiss me?"

I looked away, somewhat embarrassed.

"Most extraordinary," clicked and murmured Sodu. "Proof before us that an outsider *can* survive the connection."

"Indeed," agreed Onu. "However, we must take into account that the Commander *is* a very unique being."

"True," Sodu answered.

I couldn't help but think that it was my pleading that had miraculously brought him back.

The Commander looked at them. Onu bowed, followed by Sodu.

"The knowledge to protect your people—it will work," said the Commander. "I'm not sure how, but"—he briefly looked at the Orb—"it will."

"Yes," agreed Onu.

The Orb began to emit a faint light. I yelped and pointed. "Look!"

The light flickered on and off, repeating at different intervals.

"A reply," said Onu.

"So soon?" I queried.

"The Orb's celerity is immediate," stated Sodu. "It is connected to Tectonic energy."

Everyone stared, totally enraptured with the flickering. When it ceased, Onu and Sodu turned to the Commander and me.

"It is done," Onu announced. "The transference was successful. Our world has received the knowledge."

"Our people will now be able to prevail over the Desolators and return order to our existence," spoke Sodu.

"We must join them," said Onu, taking the staff from the Komorah. "We are indebted to you, Commander, for all that you have done, and to you, Bishop Alexandrah Hays."

"I'm glad we could be of service to you and your people," said the Commander. "Perhaps in time we will meet again."

"Perhaps," replied Onu. "However, it will not be upon this world, for we shall not return unto it. We shall in fact erase all evidence of our existence here. The city shall remain until you part from these halls." Onu touched a gem on a jeweled armband previously hidden under one of the long billowing sleeves. "Remember us well, as we will remember you. Until such time . . . good-bye."

"And good journeys to you both," Sodu finished and bowed.

A great wind gusted past the Commander and me, rippling briskly through our hair and across our clothes. Strangely the garments of the Paraxidiax Seekers and Komorah remained untouched, as if the wind was ignoring them. But contrarily, it was not ignoring them at all; rather it was unmistakably attuned to their presence, as it curiously transformed into a whirlwind around them.

"You . . . be careful out there, Bishop Alexandrah Hays . . . of Aert," the Komorah said gruffly.

"I will," I returned tearfully.

"Let the light within you shine," he said, his voice quickly fading.

In our short time together, it seemed that the great giant had grown to admire me. Perhaps it was my warrior-like bravery that had twice saved him. Perhaps it was my kindness when helping him from the sticky situation with the tuktooke pods or when using the microcellite injector to heal his wounds—or, perhaps, more than likely, it was all of these things.

The whirlwind weakened and started to dissipate. When gone, so too were the Seekers and Komorah.

"They left their Orb behind," I said.

"We'll see," said the Commander.

A few seconds later, a glow of energy formed over the Orb and the rails that encircled it. A dark metallic dome began to materialize. It then suddenly rose, revealing itself as an even larger Orb. It hovered a moment before darting up through the opening above.

"Makes me feel like we should be with them, helping," I said, looking up.

"I know," replied the Commander, putting his arm around me and attempting to catch a final glimpse. "But I think they can handle it," he finished assuredly.

I quietly agreed.

THE BEGINNING

The Commander and I walked down the steps of the library and took our last look at the various structures around us. A beam of light streamed down from the heavens and touched the tip of the spire we had noticed on our first approach into the city. The light began to sparkle, and, like a string of molten froth, the light passed downward and over the buildings and walls, over the plateaus, and around the many arches, leaving nothing in its wake. It then sparkled over the courtyard like a crest of water reaching some sandy shore and moved toward and under the Dee-Dee, up the stairs, under our feet, and up the grand columns of the library. Large sparkling shards dropped from the highpoints and melted away as they landed. The string of light then backed down and erased the grand building from sight.

In a matter of minutes the entire city simply disappeared from existence, leaving it a rocky and barren landscape. The beam of light retracted back into the heavens. A distinct and familiar smell of ozone was the only thing left behind. The Paraxidiax Seekers had indeed kept their word as to erasing all evidence of their existence.

"Wow," I uttered in amazement.

"Mm, supernal geomolecular disintegration," said the Commander pretentiously, making it sound like it wasn't all that amazing as he sat on what were, just moments before, the steps of the library.

I sat beside him. "I think you just make this stuff up."

"No," he defended.

"I think you do."

"No, it's true."

"Really?"

"Really," he assured.

We stared outward.

"Commander," I uttered thoughtfully and paused.

"*Yessss,*" the Commander replied, continuing in another dramatic overtone. "*Once* again you *burn* with question and *thirst* for answer! I can tell."

"Sounds like something Claire would say," I said.

"How would you know?" asked the Commander.

"Oh, I know her better than you think," I responded mysteriously.

"Do you now?"

I grinned briefly and continued with my burning question. "You—you said that you were there, that you made it happen, about the Desolators being no more. What happened?"

The Commander fixed his eyes toward the horizon. I could see that the question held great pain for him.

"That, my dear Bishop, is a story for another time," he replied softly.

As a gust of wind blew over us, I combed my hand through my hair, pushing it from my eyes. I brushed my hand over the duty-recorder that was still attached to my temple. I had forgotten it was there—forgotten that I had left it recording. I removed it and looked at it, cherishing the good and the bad that it held. I pressed a button.

"Re-re-record-ord-ord-ording co-o-o-or-cor-cor-cor-corrupted," the voice from it crackled.

"Oh no!" I cried. "It's all lost!"

To my disappointment, there was nothing to prove where we had been or what we had done—no evidence of my adventures to take back home, no mention of my name to be made in the *Space Exploration Journals*, and certainly no specially constructed starships to come here. Charley wanted me to record something amazing for him, and now it was gone.

I looked out toward the now barren landscape. Even if there was evidence, there was no place to return to, I thought—just rocks and wind and . . . *crystals!* There were oxygen-producing crystals! I looked around. These too were gone; obliterated by the beam of light. But I still had one contained in the vacuum vial. I pulled it out from my belt.

Further disappointment. The vial was cracked, and the crystal within had almost completely evaporated. During my fall, when escaping from the museum, I must have landed sharply on the pouch containing the vial. Despite this, I grinned.

The Commander was looking at me and had read my expression. "You still want to see what's out there?" he asked inquisitively.

"Of course," I replied. "This is just the beginning."

"Desolators are out there," he reminded me.

"We'll have to be even more vigilant, then," I said with confidence.

"True." He bounced up suddenly. "So where were we off to, anyway?" he questioned cheerfully.

"Foram . . . something," I replied.

"Oh, yes—*Foramjuruit!*"

"Yeah." I smiled.

The Commander offered a hand to help me to my feet. I took it willingly.

"First we need to return the prince to his realm!" he said as we jogged down the rocky hill and toward the Dee-Dee.

"It'll be good to see him reunited with his people," I said.

"There shall be a joyous feast for such an occasion, I expect!" the Commander proclaimed.

As the Commander entered the Dee-Dee, I stopped, crouched down, and grabbed a rock from the ground. *Maybe something yet valuable,* I thought. Maybe it held something unique within its makeup—something rare, or better yet, something undocumented. If not, it was at least a souvenir.

I looked toward the top of the hill. A pleasant light was brewing over the once dark side of the horizon, as if it were wishing us a kind farewell and good journeys ahead.

"You comin'?" hollered the Commander.

"Yep," I replied.

I then dashed up the ramp.

May peace and great strength be with you.

The Farewell to *LSC Terra Nova*
The late King Dafydd, the Orator
AM 7117 (AD 3113)

CPSIA information can be obtained at www.ICGtesting.com
Printed in the USA
LVOW11*1225050914

402603LV00002B/3/P